The Descendant

The Descendant

By Prophet
Jamal Johnson

ISBN: Hardcover   978-1-5434-6339-2
               Softcover   978-1-5434-6338-5
               eBook   978-1-5434-6337-8

Print information available on the last page.

Rev. date: 11/07/2017

To order additional copies of this book, contact:
Xlibris
1-888-795-4274
www.Xlibris.com
Orders@Xlibris.com
770009

Contents

Dedications

This book is dedicated to...
God for giving me the ability to write and express my vision in a way that can impact the lives of my readers. Nothing is possible without you and I am grateful to you for you many blessings and favor.

Jesus Christ, through whose sacrifice we can receive eternal life. You lived your life as an example for us to follow and I pray that my words and actions constitute what you stood for by spreading your message and creating disciples.

Acknowledgements

To my lovely wife Eboni Johnson who has supported me and sacrificed so much so that I can succeed in my endeavors. I truly could not have done it without you.

To Angela Barrett for encouraging my writing and showing me that blood has no bearing on true family.

To my best friends Stanchele Winchester and Taurian Monegan for always believing in me and supporting everything I did.

To my brother J.C Collins for also encouraging my writing and helping me establish myself as a writer at a young age.

To my friend Dave Nickerson for guiding me through the foundation of God's word, without understanding I would not

be able to incorporate scripture's teachings in my writing.

To my cousin Linda Nelson for being a mother to me and always loving and supporting me.

To my Aunt Alfreda Shelton and Cousin Daniel Shelton for your constant encouragement, love and support.

To the Lyrical Entertainment Ministries Team, everyone who had a hand in making this book come to fruition; from the editors, publishers, distributors, and anyone else who was a part of this amazing process. Especially my brother Henry Johnson Jr. & my dear friend Mr. William Lince and the rest of my family and friends, thank you.

Lastly, to my father Henry Johnson for showing me what it truly means to be a father, the examples you set in my life made writing Jesus's character as a father so much easier. I will never forget what you taught me, until we meet again thank you.

Prologue:

The Crucifixion

Have you ever felt as if there was a dark cloud drifting overhead on a sunny day? As if the bright rays from the sun itself still could not shield you from the horrible feeling you carry inside? It was morning, we had arrived at Golgotha (which means "the place of the skull,") and I found myself trying to remember those most subtle, yet precious moments with my father. You see, my mother and the others had watched as my father was taken out from Pilate's palace by the Roman solders, Pharisees, and other Jewish leaders. We followed alongside him with the crowd as we traveled all the way here from the city. They beat him, spat on him, and forced him to carry this immensely large wooden cross on his back until they forced a man from the crowd to carry it behind him. His clothes were tattered, stained with dried blood that seemed to paint the portrait of torture. The only thing more apparent than the dried bloodstains was the fresh bloodstains from each blow to the face and body. They had placed a crown of thorns on his head, each thorn jagged as it ripped into the skin like that of a shearing knife skinning the catch of suppers hunt. At the time, I could not fully understand what was happening, or what was to happen soon after. Father just kept moving praying aloud for their forgiveness. As we walked, I just prayed to God for everything to be all right. The Roman soldiers mocked him as they walked, accompanied by others who did not accept father's teaching. They too had insulted him with words, announcing to the crowd that this must come to pass because it was God's will that he should be crucified for his blasphemy. After we arrived, the Roman soldiers kept the crowd at bay as they began to prepare the site. We all had fallen behind; I stayed close to mother while the others continued to walk up ahead through the crowd. The air became thick; I felt a sharp pain in my chest as if small pieces of shattered glass were filling up in my lungs as I attempted to breathe in. I looked up at my mother and saw the tears begin to gather in her eyes once more, as she held me closer. The shouting from the crowd was terrifying, I just stood there, my hands clinging tightly to her cloak, my fingers intertwined with the material as if it provided relief of the morning's terror. I wanted to ask if father was ok, because I could not see over the men in front of us, for the crowd was vast.

"Look at you now!" they yelled at him. "You said you were going to destroy the Temple and rebuild it in three days. Well then, if you are the Son of God, save yourself and come down from the cross!"

I looked over to grandmother and Uncle John and thought to myself, "Why do these people hate him so?"

A few of my mother's tears landed on my forehead, they were warm, gentle, like soft raindrops in the spring. Suddenly my mind left me and my body began to move on its own. Unconsciously, I found myself letting go of my mother's cloak and began to run through the crowd, crawling in between legs and squeezing myself between the adults.

I could hear mother call out, "Yeshai, come back!" As she attempted to come after me.

I continued to navigate my way through the crowd, and then suddenly- I heard a faint voice.

"Why do you run to your father? Do you not understand that all of this must come to pass?" The voice softly whispered to me as if their lips were resting against my right earlobe, it seemed familiar to me but I could not remember where I heard it before.

At that very moment, I saw a child, a little girl standing ahead of me, smiling as if she knew who I was. She reached out her hand;

"You do not understand, but soon you will." The voice whispered again as I looked into her eyes intently while extending out my hand.

Taking it, she pulled me through to the front of the crowd with so much force that I stumbled and fell.

"Yeshai! His mother exclaimed as she helped him to his feet, letting go of his hand.

"Huh, wait, where is the little girl?" I asked mother as I looked around behind me to the crowd, she was now gone.

"I never let go of her hand, how did she vanish? Now mother's hand is what had me." I thought to myself as I attempted to make sense of what just happened. My mind quickly began to fill with questions like where did the she go, who was she, and what does all of this mean?

"Sabella, take Yeshai and go over to Mary, he does not need to witness this." *John told her as he ran out of the crowd behind us.*

"Uncle John, I want to see my father, did you hear the little girl's voice too? I asked him.

Mother took my head and placed it close to her hip and she began to walk with me trying to shield the view up ahead as John followed closely behind us. As we got closer to grandmother, I could see her crying and praying.

"My son! God give me strength!" *Mary cried.*

I could see more of father's disciples standing with her, I did not understand why mother did not want me to see father.

"What was happening to him?" I thought to myself, trying to maneuver my head around rebelliously to get a peek.

"Oh Sabella, my child come here." *Mary stated as she began opening her arms to embrace mother.*

Uncle John kneeled down in front of me and placed his hand on my head, "Everything will be ok young one, and God has a plan for all of us." He explained with watery eyes giving me a slight smile in an attempt to hide his personal grief.

I could tell he was sad, I often noticed when Uncle John was troubled. For we have always had a close understanding, my father would often remind me that he loved Uncle John dearly and that I could trust him without question. Then I heard that voice again, "Look, look at your father." the faint whisper instructed.

I tried to look past Uncle John but he continued to block my view, in the process of trying to get a view of father I saw a Roman solider walk past with a staff in hand.

"Uncle John please step aside, there is a voice telling me to look." I attempted to explain to him.

"A voice, for I did not hear any voice just now." He rebutted.

I looked up at him strangely, "Could he not hear the voice?" I thought.

A mysterious force pushed Uncle John aside, and there I was standing there with my head down in front of where they had my father. I could see the shadow of father's cross engulf me; I had finally reached him but was afraid to look up.

"Yeshai my son, its ok, look up" My father's voice softly screeched.

I gathered my strength and slowly looked up and there he was hanging. His arms and feet nailed to this enormous cross, with a sign above his head reading, "This is the king of the Jews." Alongside of him were two other men, I could hear one of them calling out to my father, hurling insults.

"Aren't you the Messiah? Save yourself and us." The man shouted.

The other man to my father's right rebuked him instantly saying;

"Don't you fear God? Since you are under the same penalty. We are being punished according to the unspeakable deeds we have done, but this man is innocent. The man exclaimed as my father's expression sluggishly began to change.

"If this man knew that my father was innocent, then why couldn't the others?" I thought to myself once more as the man to the right of my father continued.

"Jesus, remember me when you come into your kingdom." He humbly asked.

"Truly I tell you; today you will be with me in paradise!" My father answered as a slight smile slowly came across his face.

It was at that moment that I worried not for my father's fate, but instead found solace that someone in such a grim situation would ask him something like that. My mother attempted to walk towards us but Uncle John grabbed and held her.

"We mustn't interfere with God's will, I felt God move me out of Yeshai's way, so this must come to pass." He explained.

For I was just a boy, who traveled from place to place with our family and the other followers of my father. He would sometimes go off to faraway lands with his disciples while mother and I remained at home. There was much yet to be revealed to me, I could briefly recall moving from village to village, town to town, and city to city just to find myself here at the end. Father turned back towards me and smiled, my eyes began to overflow with tears, and I attempted to construct a smile from the grim expression of sadness and fear I carried. I knew that my father was ready as he gently smiled with assurance and gave me a nod.

"Do you understand now?" The mysterious voice appeared again.

"Yes." I replied as I gathered myself to turn around and to walk back towards my mother and Uncle John.

As I began to turn, I could see a beautiful pearl white dove fly over and land on the right side of my father's cross. The little girl then came from behind the cross holding it, her right arm wrapped around its base and her left hand gently placed against his left leg. She had a pleasant face, reminded me of my mother or Aunt Mary in a way. We had been walking all morning, although I could not fully tell since the adrenaline kept my legs from staggering. It was about noon, and I could still see the dove and the little girl near father. The Dove flew away and the girl faded away into the wind, as the clouds began to converge overhead. The sunlight dispersed behind the clouds, one would think while looking up into the sky that the sun itself was being stripped of its light. For hours the darkness lingered, a very still silence was sharply broken from the men's cries of agony.

"Why not just kill them, why continue to let them suffer?" A man from the crowd yelled.

"No, let them suffer, two rebels and a blasphemer who claims to be greater than Moses deserve nothing less!" Another man countered.

I could hear the faint sobs of Aunt Mary as she sat on the ground curled up in an infant's position at grandmother's feet. Peter was pacing back and forth next to us in a frantic panic, he looked upset but yet hurt as if he had just gotten his heart broken by a loved one. Although I did not know the extent of that feeling, I innocently assumed it was something similar to the time when a dog I befriended was killed. I could see almost everyone off in the distance of the crowd, all except Judas Iscariot. Since he held the money, I thought he would be somewhere close by.

"Maybe he was tending to matters of money or maybe purchasing food for the poor as I've seen him do before. But why at a time like this would he not be here?" I tried to figure out while scratching my head.

"How could I betray my Lord, I know Rabbi told us that this would come to pass but I can't help but feel responsible. Am I just as unworthy as Judas?" *Peter mumbled quietly to himself as conviction and grief began to take him.*

I could not make out what Peter was saying but I could tell that something was wrong with him. The other disciples along with mother and grandmother began to pray, and then I heard father cry out to God as the wind began to blow.

"My God, my God, why have you forsaken me?" Jesus exclaimed.

The people started talking amongst themselves, some said that he was calling Elijah, while others questioned if he was in fact the Messiah. A Roman soldier ran up to him with a sponge and gave father a drink. Father looked over to Uncle John and grandmother;

"Woman, here is your son." He told grandmother, and to Uncle John, "Here is your mother." They both nodded in agreement, as their eyes began to flow rivers of tears.

"My love, daughter of man, you know what you must do. I entrust our son to you, farewell." He lovingly declared.

After saying this father simply said, "It is finished."

I then saw my mother fall to the ground in tears and began to shake hysterically.

"My love, my love, my heart, no, no, no, my Lord!" Mother cried out as father's head dropped and he lay suspended and motionless.

Grandmother, Uncle John, Aunt Mary and a few other disciples ran over to hold her as I stood in a state of shock, my father - was dead. Suddenly the ground began to shake terribly; the massive trembling of the land caused some people to fall to the ground. In a huge panic everyone fled, people were shouting that surely Jesus was the son of God as they retreaded down the hill. Everyone in our group just held together during the earthquake, we prayed together until it subsided. After the ordeal was over a few of us began to walk away weeping while myself Uncle John, mother, and grandmother stayed a moment to mourn father.

"Uncle John, what are those Roman soldiers doing to father?" I asked softly for I felt weak and lightheaded.

He turned to me and pointed to the soldiers spear, as he plunged it into father's side.

"They are trying to see if your father has passed." Uncle John answered.

"Commander, the one called Jesus is dead, what would you like for us to do?" the centurion asked.

Just then, he noticed that a mixture of water and blood poured down the spear.

"What is this?" *the centurion exclaimed.*

I saw the look upon his face; he was terrified as if he just realized that they had made a mistake by taking the life of my father. I could hear him mumble while looking at his hands;

"What have we done?"

"It is of no consequence, we will take them down later, for now, we are finished here." *The commander ordered as majority of the soldiers left for the city.*

"It pains me not only to lose a son, but to know that all of you are also in pain. Today has been very trying on all of us, let us leave for now; these soldiers will not release his body to us. We will petition Pilate so that we can give him a proper burial." Grandmother reluctantly explained.

Silently everyone looked at each other and acknowledge grandmother's words, so we all turned and began to head back to where we were staying for the festival. On the way down form Golgotha, we saw a man named Joseph who told us that he had received permission to retrieve father's body. We gave thanks to God knowing that we could bury him with honor, and that God's will had been done. The darkened sunset, the crust from our eyes and noses flaked off into the wind as Uncle John, Peter, and a few other disciples headed back up the hill with Joseph. Have you ever felt as if there was a dark cloud drifting overhead on a sunny day? As if the bright rays from the sun still could not shield you from the horrible feeling you carried inside. I have felt such pain, I have seen such tragedy, but I have also seen miracles, I have laid witness to God's will become complete, I was blessed to know the Messiah, Jesus Christ of Nazareth - I have seen my father.

To those whom great responsibility is given, even more responsibility is required.
-Prophet

Chapter 1:

The Prodigy

T he day was gloomy as clouds covered the sky, it was as if night and day had fought a fierce battle which came to a halting stalemate. The wind blew across the plains with the soft echo of a swirling whistle as I began to walk down the grassy path to fetch water from the river. We lived in a small tent near the Jordan River east of the town of Nazareth and Mt. Tabor, which overlooked the mouth at which the river opened into the Sea of Galilee. Father was building our home; there were piles of wood, stone, and hay surrounding the area next to our tent. Father was very good with his hands, last year he carved me a wooden horse as a present for my 7th birthday. My favorite toy, its eyes were polished to a slight shimmer but somehow kept this fierce expression as if it was riding into war. I carried it in my left hand and the wooden bucket father had made in my right, that horse was more like an extremity than a toy as I took it everywhere with me. When I arrived at the river, I sat the bucket down, picked up one of the small rocks, and tossed it across. It was smooth and oval shaped, and skipped off the surface of the water once, twice, three times before submitting to the current's momentum and was submerged.

"Darn, I'll make it all the way across next time." I muttered aloud to myself as I slapped my thigh and picked up the bucket.

"Yeshai, hurry and bring the water back so I can begin making supper." Mother called out to me from the house.

She could always tell when I was up to mischief; I could never get anything past her. So with haste I filled the bucket and ran back up to the house, the toy wooden horse tightly in hand.

Across the river as Yeshai had gathered water to take home, a hooded figure emerged from the forest and walked to the riverbank watching intently as he returned home to his parents.

"Interesting, very interesting." *The hooded figure sinisterly expressed. Beneath his hood, only a villainous smirk accompanied by a pair of misty red eyes could be seen as he stepped back into the forest.*

As I arrived back at the tent I could see mother preparing supper, she was chopping vegetables for the rabbit stew. The small fire was ready to start boiling the water, and I always enjoyed mothers cooking. Father would often tell me that her cooking was one of the many things he loved about her.

"Were you down by the river throwing rocks again?" Mother inquired with an intense glare. "Never mind I know you were, trying to make it all the way across again I presume, my strong boy." She jokingly giggled.

"Yes, mother." I replied with a dry sarcastic snarl, she knew making fun of me drove me crazy.

"Well it will be a little while before supper is ready, go and see if your father needs help building." She kindly instructed me.

I walked over to where my father was building the house; well it was not much of a house just yet being that there were only two walls and a window. Father was placing the stone and mortar to begin on the third wall when he looked up and saw me approaching.

"Son, hand me that hammer." My father instructed as he began to put one of the building stones in place.

"Mother said for me to help you because supper won't be ready for a little while." I told him.

I had helped father build things before, he would show me where to cut, how to measure, and which tools to use. I loved the time we spent together, even if it was just a simple fishing trip out on the riverbank or on the crystal waters of the sea.

"Did she now?" He replied with a smirk. "Very well we should be able to make some progress before the food is ready."

Jesus took one of the stones and handed it to Yeshai.

"Father, are we still going to see grandmother tomorrow?" I excitingly asked as my eyes opened wide in anticipation.

"Yes I suppose that will be alright." He slowly agreed as to build up the suspense.

Father always loved keeping someone is suspense, but this time it did not matter. I saw his amusing games as a well-awaited opportunity to take a visit to grandmother's house. There were other children there to play with, one of which being my best friend Naomi. Ever since grandfather died, my father and I would frequently visit her to make sure she was ok and tend to any of her needs. We would always bring her grain from the local vender on the outskirts of town so she would not have to make the trip alone. Soon after he passed she stayed with us for a short time, father told her that she should consider living with us once he finished the house but stubbornly she refused. She would always say that Nazareth was her home and she did not want to leave. She was a very strong willed woman and loving, she could to turn your most dreadful mood into something truly exceptional. I loved my grandmother, her and my mother were very close. One time we received word that grandmother had gotten very ill while father was away purchasing supplies for the house. Mother packed our belongings, left a note for father and off we were to grandmothers at once. We stayed with her for three weeks while mother nursed her back to health.

"Yeshai!" Father exclaimed pulling my attention back to him.

"Your head is always in the clouds, take a moment, and focus son. Let us finish this so we can eat supper."

I often get lost in thought where my mind just fades, leaving my body in limbo as my thoughts race across my conscience. I looked up at him with an apologetic expression that quickly turned into a smile. There was a quiet pause, we faced each other and burst into laughter.

"Let me use the hammer father." I giggled.

Yeshai and his father laughed and talked as they worked as the sun began to set. Sabella came over to them, kissed Yeshai on the forehead before sitting down on Jesus's lap.

"My love, supper is ready so you and Yeshai get yourselves cleaned up and let's eat." *She said gently stroking his hair with her fingertips.*

I just sat and observed them, I did not fully understand the concept of "true love" but I was sure of one thing, whatever it was, they were it. They always expressed their love for one another; mother was father's precious jewel. As they sat there looking into each other's eyes I said quietly to myself;

"I want that for me one day."

Mother stood up, softly took father's hand, and started walking towards the tent. I followed behind looking off into the distance and noticed a shadowy figure that seemed to be looking directly at me. Its eyes had an eerie red glow to them, like rubies. It was too far away to make out exactly what it was but it made me feel strange, like something bad was going to happen.

"Yeshai, come now it is time for supper!" Mother and father called out to me.

As I began to continue over to them, I quickly looked back off into the distance but the figure was gone. As I sat down I still had a strange feeling, but I attempted to put it in the back of my mind and enjoy supper with my parents.

"This smells very good Sabella; you have outdone yourself yet again." Father complimented her as she served us our plates.

We sat next to the fire as we ate; I stared into its flames. The warmth against my skin was relaxing and reassuring, placing me at ease. The crackling sound of the of the flames combined with the distant sound of the rushing waters of the Jordan as it opened into the Galilee sea made such a tranquil song. After we finished our meal father led us in prayer:

"Father in heaven, praise and glory be unto you. Your love and mercy has no equal, you are alpha and omega, the unseen ruler, and may your kingdom reign forever. Lord we give thanks for your provision tonight, for we know you will provide for us the rest of our days. May your spirit fill our hearts so that we may overflow with joy, all honor and distinction belong to you for we celebrate your name to all the lands, boasting in thankfulness of your grace, amen"

When he finished we all sat in silence for a moment giving thanks to the Lord almighty for his favor and many blessings. Father taught me how to pray, for he would often go to a quiet place to do so. Mother began putting what was left of the food away.

"Yeshai, can you help me?" She asked as the flames from the fire continued to flicker.

"Yes mother, of course." I eagerly responded, for I loved to help mother do different things because she always made me feel like I really made a difference. Both she and Grandmother Mary were both very encouraging and nurturing, I often wondered if Grandmother raised her too.

"You're always so helpful, my little man of God." She pleasantly commended me.

She always called me that, I thought it was because I spent time reading the scriptures and was very close to completing the Tora. Normally children my age would just be starting it, to have it memorized by age thirteen but not me. I managed to spend the free time I had reading when I was not playing or running errands for mother. I found reading interesting, father told me that reading was one of the ways I could get to know the heavenly father. I once asked Naomi did she believe in God, she said she did not really know because it was something she was taught to do.

Yeshai sat there next to his parents thinking about the conversation with Naomi.

"What do you mean by that?" I asked her inventively.

"I guess I mean that I really don't know what I believe in, I was told that God is out there and that I should read the scriptures and follow his commandments. My parents believe, I guess I will fully understand one day." She explained.

"Well if no one told you to believe, would you?" My questions continued persistently, I was intrigued and could not help it.

Naomi paused for a moment; you could see the intense look on her face. Her forehead cringed, three lines above her eyebrow rippled up to her hairline. With her mouth slightly tilted, she crossed her legs and she began to scratch her chin.

"Um, I do not know, I guess not." She reluctantly answered.

It really made me think;

"Did the adults have these types on conversations with each other?" My thoughts began to race.

"What about you, would you believe if no one told you to?" She sharply interrogated me in an attempt to even the playing field.

"Um, honestly yea." I slowly replied. I could not explain it to her at the time but for some strange reason I always felt a connection to God. The way the wind would blow sometimes felt like someone was calling my name. Even reading the scriptures seem to feed the insatiable hunger that I had within myself.

"You are so strange Yeshai, come on lets go play in the marketplace." *Naomi joked as she grabbed Yeshai's hand and began to run off dragging him behind her.*

"Yeshai, it is time to get some rest, we have a long day ahead of us tomorrow." Jesus told him.

The sun had completely set by now, the clouds in the sky were faint and thin, almost transparent as the light from the moon gave a distinct glow. Yeshai prepared for bed as if his father instructed and cuddled in between his parents. They both kissed him on the head and wrapped an arm around him. His thoughts attempted one last time to race, quickly he thought about the day's festivities. He thought about the strange figure he saw, the conversation with Naomi, going to see his Grandmother, and all the good talks was shared over dinner. Yeshai briefly gave a silent prayer as all of his thoughts passed away, his eyes became weighted as he finally drifted off to sleep.

"He is asleep; he is growing and growing every day." Sabella quietly mumbled to Jesus.

"Yes, he grows in the spirit just as much as he grows in knowledge and understanding. He will do great things, many will follow him." Jesus quietly mumbled in response.

"Do you know what God has planned for him?" She asked protectively.

"God has not yet revealed to me his plan and purpose for Yeshai's life. However, one thing is for sure he has the potential to have a great following. Like an anointed king over the land he will have the power and influence to guide men to the truth or turn them away from it." Jesus explained to her as he began to gently stroke Yeshai's head.

"Just look at him, so innocent and fragile, it is hard to even fathom our son being the cause of someone turning against God. We will continue to raise him up in the Lord so that he may have his favor upon him all of his days." Sabella announced as tears began to build up in her eyes.

"That we will my love; that we will. Let us not worry ourselves with thoughts of such a future, for my time has not yet come that God's glory shall be realized through me, all will be revealed in when our heavenly father decides." Jesus explained as Sabella nodded in agreement giving a slight smile as Jesus spoke.

"Yes my love you are right." She replied nodding in agreement with a slight smile.

"Come now, let us go to sleep." Jesus told her, he passionately kissed her on the lips and forehead and they lay there until they dozed off into slumber.

Our journeys in life are not orchestrated by the choices we make, for we are just leaves blowing in the wind of God.
-Prophet

Chapter 2:

A Journey Begins

*T*he sweet sound of birds chirping filled the morning sky followed by the faint splashing of the distant running water from the Jordan. Yeshai awoke and stretched out his arms and noticed that his father had gone. He reached out and placed his hand where his father laid, the fabric was cool to the touch until his hand reached where the sunlight had bypassed the tents opening. He looked over at his mother as she slept ever so peacefully, her natural slight smile rested against her hand. She was the most beautiful woman in the world to him, God's own personal grace manifested in human form. Yeshai sat up and rubbed the crust from his eyes, it was about six in the morning. He delicately kissed his mother on the forehead and headed out to look for his father.

"Where could he have gone?" I thought to myself, while anxiously scanning my head from left to right looking up into the hills for father.

I figured he was probably off praying in solitude so I decided to pack my bag to prepare for the trip to Grandmother's. Turning around I noticed that mother had awakened and started to pack father's bag.

"Your father is somewhere near; go to him so that you both may be on your way."

Mother advised pointing me in the direction of the hills near our home.

"Ok I will seek him out so we can leave, but first may I have some water, I am thirsty?" I politely asked her.

"Yes but sadly we do not have anymore; I used the last of the water you gathered yesterday on the meal I prepared. You will have to go back down to the river to get a drink, and clean yourself up while you are there, my little man of God." She replied while giving me a wink and nudging me in my arm with her elbow.

I once again picked up the bucket father made and my toy wooden horse and headed back down to the river. As I walked, I noticed that my vision had begun to get blurry and I became slightly dizzy which increased with every step the closer I got to the river.

"It's getting harder and harder to see, I must be tired or something." I thought to myself while shaking my head in an attempt to rid myself of the dizzy spell.

I noticed myself starting to stumble as I finally approached the riverbank. I fell to my knees, unable to stand up my body grew weaker and weaker as I could feel my eyes becoming harder and harder to remain open. Before my eyes clothed I could see a figure in a dark black robe sitting in front of the water with its back to me.

"What is happening to me, huh, wait, who – a – are – y - you?" I cried out groggily.

Yeshai then passed out and fell face first into the brown sand.

When I awoke, I saw the figure standing over me; I could not make out its face due to my sight not being fully regained. I mustered the remaining strength I had in an attempt to stand to my feet but to no avail. Exhausted and overwhelmed I laid there in the sand and watched the figure walk away. I could hear him say;

"Soon, very soon, we will meet again little man of God he he." The figure gave a sinister laugh as my vision turned completely black once more.

"Yeshai, son, wake up, wake up son!" Father called out to me.

"Is - is - that- you - father?" I faintly asked, my voice cracking as if my throat was dry as the sands of Egypt.

Jesus picked him up and carried him to the river. Holding Yeshai in one hand, cupping his other to dip into the water to give him a drink.

"Here, drink this." *Jesus told him.*

After a few moments of drinking Yeshai was able to stand on his own. It was almost as if his father's touch alone regained his strength.

"Father, what happened?" I asked, looking around to see if I could see the figure of in the distance.

"It appears that you fainted while fetching the water, I came down to make sure you were well." He explained as we began walking back up the riverbank.

Picking up my bucket and toy wooden horse, I looked up at father, and he looked back at me with concern. I could not fully understand it but I just had a strange feeling about everything that had happened.

"Is everything alright son, you seemed troubled?" *Jesus asked, for he knew what was happening to Yeshai, in fact he saw it night before while speaking to Sabella about his future and God's plan for him. This is why he just told her, "Let us not worry ourselves with thoughts of such a future?"*

"I'm not sure what's going on. I have had this bad feeling in my stomach, first I get these head aches and then I become very dizzy." I reluctantly replied, purposely withholding the fact that I had been seeing this shadowy figure and could not make sense of it. Who was he and what did he want? Those questions kept revolving repeatedly in my head but I just kept walking with father.

Jesus watched his demeanor closely, sensing the awkwardness he did not pry with questions about the ordeal, rather he placed his hand on the back of his son's neck in an attempt to comfort him.

"Your mother has a great remedy for headaches; she can make a batch before we leave if you are still feeling up to going to your Grandmother's?" Jesus facetiously asked him, he knew nothing would keep that boy from seeing his Grandmother and friends.

"No thank you, I should be fine." I immediately responded, planting both feet firmly in the ground. He knew nothing was going to keep me from seeing my grandmother and Naomi.

By the time they returned home, Sabella had already prepared their bags and loaded them on their colt. Yeshai's eyes grew very wide; his expression began to display the excitement he began to fill.

"We are bringing Sampson! Oh can I ride him please?" I exclaimed, I loved riding Sampson. I remember when father brought him home and mother let me name him.

I gave him the name Sampson because he had much longer hair than the average colt and was so strong, he would carry all of father's supplies from town to town with ease. When father would take food and clothing to the neighboring areas to give to the poor Sampson would gladly carry them for his favorite treat, a big plump juicy green apple.

"Sure, but not the entire journey." He sternly yet considerately answered.

Father's voice was not rough and raspy but held an authoritative tone. It was as if he always demanded respect while giving others the utmost respect simultaneously. Following scripture I always tried my best to honor my father and mother but it is easier when your father has such a powerful presence for such a humble appearance. Mother and father embraced and kissed, signaling me to come over to embrace and say goodbye. Afterwards father lifted me up and I sat down on Sampson, I could feel his robust beneath my legs and backside bouncing me up and down with every step.

"You two be safe, and may God guide and protect you on your travels. Tell mother I said hello, and that she is always in my prayers. Yeshai mind your father and don't go wandering too far off." Mother called out as she waived, our view of her became smaller and smaller as we headed up along the mouth of the Jordan.

Once we cleared the large hills along the Jordan, we headed east since it was too steep to travel directly there. My excitement continued to grow as I thought of arriving in Nazareth, my stomach was filled with an intense sensation like as if I was falling down. Father could see that I was being worked up because I had become extremely restless; I began squirming in my cloth saddle on Sampson while sighing every few minutes.

"Calm down son, it's at least a day's journey to get there since we do not travel during the night time. You are going to make it much longer working yourself up, as you do, be patient, for we will arrive at the appointed time. Come down let's give Sampson a break, we will rest here shortly." Father willfully suggested.

I nodded my head in obedience and jumped off of Sampson, father gave him a green apple and then we sat down on a large rock. I picked up a large twig that had fallen from a nearby tree and began drawing circles on the ground. This made me think of mother, and I began to miss her. She would sit with me sometimes and help me draw pictures in the sand; she always said that I could draw anything I put my mind to and that the world is a beautiful canvas that God has created just waiting to be captured.

"Father, can I ask you a question?" I gently inquired.

"You can ask me anything." He answered reassuringly.

"How did you and mother meet each other?" I continued my line of questions.

"Your mother's families were travelers, going from place to place exchanging goods and selling items they acquired along their travels. When they arrived in Nazareth, they decided to stay and settle there. I was not too much older than you were when I saw her, her beauty paled in comparison to her grace. As kids, we used play together all of the time and we became best friends, similar to you and Naomi. Instantly I thought of Naomi;

"I hope he isn't trying to make it seem like me and Naomi will be like them and get married, EW no way she is gross!" I thought to myself with a forceful frown covered my face.

Father laughed aloud profusely, leaning back against the rock slapping his knee.

"You must be thinking about you marrying Naomi ha!" He continued laughing.

I began to stare at him fiercely; it was not funny that he was laughing. Mother was normally the one who made fun with him it was always worse.

"Naomi and I, oh no that's crazy!" I immediately blurted out in defense.

"It is ok son, who knows what the Lord has in store for you two when you are older." He continued in an attempt to withhold his laughter.

"Um can we continue the trip, I think Sampson is ready to earn another apple." I quickly proposed in an attempt to change the subject.

Father just smiled and nodded his head, and we continued walking along the path to Nazareth. Sometime later I began thinking about what he said, trying to make sense of it all. Naomi and I were best friends; I have known her pretty much my entire life. I have never thought of her in any other way than a friend, in fact I have never thought of anyone in that way before. We traveled a good ways and the sun began to hide behind a cluster of clouds, giving the land an amber burnt orange color. As the sun set it began to get quiet, the sound of birds chirping no longer echoed off in the distance. All you could hear was a slight rustling of the leaves in the trees as a mild wind blew. Father told me to always pay attention to my surroundings so as we walked my eyes moved left to right scanning the area. He noticed me give out a yawn and said;

"We have traveled far enough for today; we will set up camp, get some rest, and continue on tomorrow."

"Ok I am getting a little tired." I told him as I stretched out my arms and gave another yawn.

"Tie up Sampson to the tree and give him an apple, I will start on the fire." Father instructed.

I took Sampson by his reigns and walked him over to a tree that towered over our campsite and tied them to a branch. I took our bags, removed the cloth saddle from his back, and gently petted his side. I went over and sat next to father, handing him a loaf of bread mother had packed for us to eat along our trip. He broke the bread, gave thanks, and handed me the bigger portion.

"God always provides, and besides you are a growing boy." He said giving me a warm smile.

"I want to grow up and become just like you!" I responded encouragingly as I took the first bite of my portion of bread.

Father always ate slowly, as if he cherished every bit of food. He always told me how important it was to appreciate what God provides and it showed in almost everything he did.

"Truly, one day you will understand just how important this bread is. And on that day you will think back to this moment and acknowledge God." He announced proudly with his portion of bread in one hand and the other moving as he spoke.

"What does he mean?" I silently thought to myself.

"Do not worry yourself about it now, finish eating, and rest, for we have a long journey ahead of us tomorrow." He said as he looked up at the stars intensely as if something were about to fall down. I did not understand father's words so I just replied with the first that came to mind;

"Yes father."

They both ate and were satisfied, afterwards they prayed together, laid down next to the fire, and slept until morning.

Sometimes the lessons learned along the journey are just as important as the destination.
-Prophet

Chapter 3:

The Traveler

*B*efore the sun began to climb over the horizon Jesus had already awaken and prepared Sampson for travel. Knowing Yeshai was exhausted from the trip he decided to let him sleep in. The outline of the distant mountain range began to glow amber orange as the sun attempted to come out. A slight slimmer of smoke continued to creep through the firewood and rise into the air from the ambient embers than flickered below.

"Yeshai, wake up. It is time for us to leave here and continue on." *Jesus said while gently shaking his shoulder.*

Yeshai slowly opened his eyes and let out a huge yawn.

"Is it morning already father, it's still dark outside." *Yeshai asked.*

"For the one whom beats the sun will prosper in its light, giving birth to opportunity and prosperity and the one who is beaten by the sun will fall into calamity." *Jesus explained in a parable.*

"What does that mean? It is too early for father's riddles." *Yeshai thought to himself. His face filled with confusion but he nodded as if he understood anyway as to not reveal his ignorance to the statement.*

They began walking along the path once more, this time Yeshai decided to give Sampson's back a break. They traveled across a long distance, crossed rivers and streams, and grassy plains. Yeshai looked over at his father and noticed that he had been quiet the last few miles or so and became concerned.

"Is everything alright father, what troubles you?" *Yeshai inquired.*

"Once we come to the end of this road there will be a man with a cart, he will seem pleasant and ask for a drink of water. You will give him a drink, and then he will ask for a bit of food, you will give him one of the loaves your mother prepared for us. Then he will thank you, turn to me, and pull out a sword and say that he will take Sampson from us. When he does this you will stand behind me and draw on the ground with your finger the word forgiveness." *Jesus carefully explained.*

Yeshai was stunned and bewildered as his father spoke, he scratched his head but listened intensely out of respect.

"How do you know this will happen?" *Yeshai reluctantly asked as if not to offend.*

"For I saw it before the sun rose over the mountains, God showed it to me in a dream." *Jesus calmly answered.*

Yeshai thought about what his father had told him while they walked. He could not wrap his head around the idea of knowing the future. A few hours later, the path that they traveled along was ending and off in the distance was a fork in the road. At this fork was a man standing next to a large cart, the cart's wheel seemed to be broken, and the man seemed to be stranded.

"Is this the man and the cart father warned me about earlier?" *Yeshai asked himself.*

As they arrived at the fork, Jesus waived over to the stranger.

"Hello friend!" *The stranger called out.*

I looked at him cautiously and remembered what father had told me.

"He will seem pleasant." *Yeshai recalled.*

The man reached out and shook my father's hand, nothing about him seemed suspicious.

"I apologize if this may be any trouble to you two but I seem to be in trouble, for the wheel on my cart is broken and I cannot travel without the goods I am supposed to sell in the town of Nazareth. I have been stuck for hours trying to fix the wheel, and have run out of drink, do you have any water to spare?" The man asked.

I walked over to Sampson and pulled out the water I had to give him a drink.

"Thank you sir for your kindness." He smiled as I handed the sheepskin flask.

I turned to father as he drank in absolute amazement but remained silent, father just nodded to me for no words needed to be said.

"Excuse me, your graciousness has gone unopposed in these troubling times, and I truly appreciate it. Do you by chance have any food to eat because I am weak from being stranded with no food?" He sincerely asked us.

Father turned to me and nodded his head once more, this time with a smile on his face. I then grabbed a loaf of bread and one of Sampson's green apples and handed it to the man. He took them and smiled at us, and then walked over to his cart.

"You two are miracles from heaven to have been on the same road as me out in this heat stranded with no food or water.

"Do you mean the cart full of food, water, and other supplies that you have right there?" Father asked him.

The man looked at father with a face of confusion, I know he was probably wondering how father knew what he had.

"Unfortunately I will have to add your colt to my collection, he looks very strong like he could carry this cart all the way to Egypt if need be. I appreciate your kindness I do but we all have to survive and make a living, so it's your colt and supplies or your life!" The man threatened, pulling a sword from the back of the cart.

I quickly ran and stood behind father, I had never been in harm's way before. My heart began to pound I could feel it beating through my shirt. Then I recalled what father told me to do and began to write on the ground with my finger the word forgiveness.

"You do not have to rob or steal, for God provides provision to all of his children." Father assured him with his hands out as if to embrace the man.

"Stand back! All I want is your supplies and colt; do not come any closer referring to God. What has God ever provided for me?" The man snapped swinging his sword wildly in an attempt to intimidate father from advancing further.

"God has provided for you Bassam, he provided for you and your mother for months after your father died." Father explained stepping closer and closer.

"What is father doing?" I thought to myself.

"H-how do you know my name? Who are you? My mother and I are none of your business!" he exclaimed.

"Oh but you are my business, you think God had abandoned you to live on the street. He heard every one of your prayers, he counted every one of your tears, and he loves you dearly." Father continued.

I looked down at the ground and realized that out of panic and adrenaline I had etched the word forgiveness in the ground so hard that my fingertips began to bleed right underneath the nail. As father got closer the man began to weep, and his hands began to shake.

"How do you know of my prayers, God did abandon us and now I'm all alone?" He said sobbingly.

"Yeshai come here. Bassam it is not your fault that your mother passed away, it was a part of God's plan for your life. I know your pain but understand the solution is to let God into your heart and casting out those rebellious feelings you hold inside. For you are not alone, he is always with you, give me the sword, it is alright, there is no need to fear me." Father gently explained to him causing the man to weep while reaching out his hand to take the sword.

I began walking over to father, by the time I got there, the man had let go of the sword and fell to his knees weeping at father's feet. I watched as father tossed the sword over to the side and embraced the man.

"It is alright, my son has something to show you. Yeshai take his hand and walk him over to where you were standing." Father instructed.

Bassam took my hand and slowly walked over to where I was standing. His eyes were red from the tears and his face was sweaty as if he had been working in the hot summer's sun. He looked down and saw the word I had written in the dirt and wept aloud. I looked over at father and without a word; I began to understand what he was trying to show me.

"Sir, God has forgiven you." I told him as I placed my hand against his leg.

Bassam wiped the tears from his eyes, turned over to father, and smiled.

"What now, what do I do now?" he asked.

"Turn from your wicked ways, follow his commands and the Lord will guide you along the way." Father calmly commanded.

"Yes, I will no longer travel down this path of unrighteousness. May God deal with me ever so severely should I not uphold this oath I give today!" Bassam announced.

"Praise be to the almighty God today for another one of his lost sons has rejoined the kingdom of heaven!" Father praised as he raised his hands.

It was amazing to me that father could show such kindness to someone who would do us harm and rob us. I looked down at my hands, those dirty bloody fingertips of mine. They had suffered and bled to give a message to this man, a message of forgiveness. I began to realize that sometimes in life you have to make sacrifices to achieve success.

"But how did you know all of those things about me?" Bassam asked.

"The Lord almighty told me, he told me that we would meet and he told me what would happen." Father replied.

"Are you a prophet? My mother told me stories of the great prophet Elijah when I was a child." He asked.

"What is it that you believe I am; truly I tell you for a prophet is just one who is chosen by God to be his messenger and voice among his people." Father asked him.

"I do not know but surely you are one chosen by God, how else would you know these things. I am grateful to have met you rabbi, what is your name?" Bassam asked as he walked over to his cart.

"Jesus of Nazareth and this is my son Yeshai." Father told him.

"What an honor it is to meet you, I apologize for before." He added.

"No apology necessary, all is forgiven. I can see that the wheel on your cart is broken, I am a carpenter, Yeshai and I can help fix it so you can be on your way." Father told him placing his hand on my shoulder.

Bassam's face glowed with a combination of appreciation and the sweat that drenched down his face. We helped him fix the tire to the wagon, and as a token of appreciation, he offered to give us some food and water but father refused.

"Although the gesture is kind, those supplies were stolen so we cannot accept them. Just go in peace and give what you have to the poor and to the widows. Do for others what was done for you today." Father told him.

Bassam respectfully nodded and left heading down the road to the right at the fork.

"God bless you Yeshai and Jesus of Nazareth, and may we meet again one day." Bassam called out as he waived his hand to us.

We waived back and continued on our journey along the road to the left of the fork towards Nazareth.

"Father, how did you know those things?" I humbly asked.

"There are things you have yet to understand but I will share with you this. God speaks to me, he tells me things and shows me things, but that is all you should concern yourself with at the moment. I know you have many questions, and you will have an answer to them but not yet. The father knows all things and has given all things to his son, and at the appointed time the son will glorify the father." He vaguely explained to me.

The questions in my head made it feel like it was going to swell up and burst, but at least father told me something. I thought the last thing he told me was just another one of his riddles; I did not understand that he was referring to his relationship to God in both likeness and in stature. By this time the sun was beginning it is decent onto the clouds in the west, I could see the outskirts of Nazareth off in the distance.

"I can see it father!" I exclaimed, it always made me happy to arrive at our destination.

"Yes son, we are almost there.

As the sunset, Yeshai climbed on the back of Sampson and rode him all the way to Nazarene border. There they walked until they reached the house of Mary, the mother of Jesus and knocked on the door.

Forgiveness is like picking a beautiful red rose, hard to achieve due to the sharp thorns that protect it. But if you can withstand the pain and the bloody fingers, you can obtain it.
-Prophet

Chapter 4:

Reality Check

*T*he sun crept between the mountain range off in the distance and its dim light completely faded out as the moon began climb up above the clouds. The stars began to appear as the fireflies that flew around mimicked their light. Yeshai excitedly waited for Mary to come to the door, he was exhausted but it had been a good while since he had seen his Grandmother.

"Grandma! We are here!" *Yeshai cried out with anticipation.*

Yeshai began to jump up and down as the sound of footsteps got louder. Mary opened the door and was immediately tackled by Yeshai, almost knocking her to the ground.

"My, oh my, someone is happy to see me!? Yeshai my very special boy, it is wonderful to see you again!" *Mary told him as she attempted to gain her footing back.*

"I've missed you!" *Yeshai exclaimed as the grip on his embrace began to tighten.*

"Yeshai, son let your Grandmother breathe, you won't have much of a Grandmother left soon if you don't relax." *Jesus said jokingly as he began to chuckle.*

"Let me have a look at you." *She told Yeshai as he let go and stood in front of her standing as tall as he could. He poked out his chest and balled up his fists as if this would enhance the appeal to her.*

"Oh how you have grown, pretty soon you will be as tall as your mother and I." *She politely patronized him, Yeshai's face lit up like the Fireflies flying nearby outside the window.*

Jesus walked up behind Yeshai and placed his hand on his head.

"Yes, he has grown quite a bit. It's so nice to see you Mother." He said with a smile.

Mary walked over and embraced Jesus, and for a moment time seemed to stand still.

"You two must be starving, there is still some food left over from the dinner I prepared. Come and sit down and tell me about your journey here." Grandmother insisted.

Father just nodded and we all sat down to eat.

"So how is Sabella doing? She must come with you next time, how I miss her so!" *Mary inquired placing her hands together with an encouraged smile on her face.*

"She is well, she send her love." Father replied.

"Mother misses you too; she talks about you all the time!" I eagerly added, being around her always made me excited.

By this time the sun had completely set and the moonlight's glow entered quietly through the window and creeping through the cracks in the door.

"How is everyone doing?" Father asked.

"Things are different here, Rome's influence has stretched out this far. People are very angry and there has been word from Jerusalem that violence has occurred." *Mary reluctantly mentioned turning her head to the window.*

"Don't worry mother, for God's will for his people transcends Rome." He told her in encouragement.

"Why are the people angry?" I asked the both of them.

There was a moment of silence as they stared at each other and then they turned to me.

"Not everyone believes in the God of Abraham, Isaac, and Jacob my precious boy. This causes confusion, especially when someone who does not believe is in power. Rome doesn't understand our beliefs so they do not respect them, which can make people angry." She tried explaining to me.

"Not everyone believes in God?" I asked in shock.

For it never occurred to me that there were people who did not believe in God. I had never seen anyone in my life or heard of it before.

"Yes son, there are people who do not accept the way of the Father. Now that you are aware of this, pray for them that they may come to the truth." Father instructed.

"Yes father, are you angry?" I asked.

"No I am not angry; my heart weeps for those who do not know the Father because it is desire that everyone knows him." He explained.

Mary looked troubled as she stood up to prepare the place where we would sleep; they could see her concern for the well-being of the people.

"Well it is late; we should rest and get ready for day ahead." Father said as he began to yawn.

I could feel my body shutting down; all of the adrenaline from seeing Grandmother had begun to fade. Traveling here actually took a toll on me; I could only imagine how Sampson felt.

After evening prayer, Yeshai lie down and immediately fell asleep. Jesus covered him with a blanket and came back over the table to sit down with his mother.

"How is Yeshai doing?" *Mary asked placing her hands on top of Jesus's.*

"He is doing well, growing everyday both physically and in the spirit. The Father has anointed him and it is shows in his action as well as in his questions." *Jesus responded.*

"Questions, what kind of questions?" She inquired.

"He has had general questions lately, some of which lead to God's plan for him. I know he is not ready to know everything but I cannot fully deny his understanding. He saw the spirit move on our way here with a man along the road whose intentions were originally for evil but God decided to be glorified instead. He saw first-hand what the love, compassion, and mercy of God could achieve." *He explained.*

"Praise God, I can see an anointing on him, I can only imagine how curious that whole ordeal made him. It is difficult as a parent to know your child has a calling that he is not ready to know yet. Jacob and I were just average people whom the Lord chose as caretakers, we did not know how to handle every situation, but we did the best we could. Yeshai will have many questions; you will know which ones to answer because you are Lord." *Mary explained as she bowed her head.*

Jesus took his hand, placed it beneath her chin and gently raised her head to eye level and smiled at her.

"Dear woman, both you and Jacob were chosen by the Father to care for me, but not by coincidence you two were destined to carry out God's will. You have done a marvelous thing in my upbringing; you are my mother whom I love dearly. Thank you for your kind words of wisdom." *Jesus gently told her while softly stroking her chin with his fingertips.*

Mary's eyes shimmered as the water from here tears began to build up, with the closing of her eye lids released a flow of tears similar to that of a river. She sat quietly for a moment and wept while still holding the hand of Jesus.

"Rejoice, for tears of joy are like the first flower that blooms in the spring." *Jesus said as he embraced her.*

"Thank you, I could have not have asked for a better son." *Mary said sobbing with a smile as he wiped away her tears.*

After their conversation, they both went to bed. The next morning Mary was the first to awake and prepared breakfast. She was filled with such a joy that her cheeks began to get sore from smiling. After she finished she opened the cloth curtain and woke them up.

"Good morning, come and eat for I have prepared breakfast!" *She exclaimed lovingly with a smile.*

Yeshai awoke and jumped onto his father.

"Father, wake up, Grandmother prepared breakfast!" *Yeshai said excitingly.*

"Now, now, what is the meaning of all of the energy this morning with the two of you?" *He replied wiping his eyes.*

"Come now son today is a day that the Lord our God has made!" *She said taking his hands and helping him to his feet.*

"Yes father, let us eat." *Yeshai teased.*

They all sat at the table, ate, and were satisfied. Afterwards they gave thanks and prayed.

"Grandmother, have you seen Naomi lately?" I asked while bouncing in my seat.

"Why yes, I saw here just the other day. She was helping her mother in the fields; I believe they will be there today as well." Grandmother answered.

"Father, may I go and play with Naomi?" I asked as father laughed.

He looked at me for a moment, and I knew exactly what he was thinking. He was making fun of me from our conversation about Naomi along the road here.

"Sure son, you may go. Send our greetings to her mother and father." He said looking over at Grandmother.

Yeshai cleaned up and ran outside and down the road towards the field, as he passed by Sampson he yelled, "Hey Sampson, and see you later!"

When he arrived at the fields, he saw Naomi off in the distance working with her mother.

"Naomi!" I yelled while trying to catch my breath.

Naomi looked up and as soon as she realized it was Yeshai immediately ran towards him.

"Yeshai!" She screamed back.

They met near the middle next to a stack of barley and hugged each other.

"I didn't know you were coming!" She exclaimed trying to catch her breath.

"Yes, father and I made it here last night. How are you?" I asked still trying to recover.

"I am great, and yourself?" She answered.

"I am great too, can we go and play?" I replied.

"Sure, let me go and ask mother." She said grabbing my hand and leading me over to her mother.

As we approached, her mother looked at me and smiled. She was always nice to me, her father as well. They seemed to like me; maybe it was because they have known me since I was a baby and knew my parents since before we were born.

"Well hello there Yeshai, it's very nice to see you again." Her mother said with a genuine smile.

"It is very nice to see you as well ma'am. My father and Grandmother sends there greetings." I shuttered nervously.

"Oh wonderful, how are they and is your mother here too?" She replied.

"They are well, and not this time she had to stay behind." I said digging my heel into the dirt and swayed from side to side.

"Aw that's too bad, well maybe next time I do enjoy our talks. Well I imagine you to want to go off and play am I right?" She rhetorically mentioned placing her hands on her hips.

We both looked up at her with the most innocent yet devious expressions we could muster.

She just laughed and shook her head, "Go, and have fun. Naomi makes sure you are home for supper, you are welcome to join us Yeshai with permission of course."

"Yes ma'am." We both eagerly responded as our feet began moving in the other direction.

Before you know it, we were sprinting in the opposite direction towards the town square. I was so occupied with excitement on seeing Grandmother and playing with Naomi that I did not even think to bring my toy wooden horse.

"Oh well, I'll get it later. I wonder what we will do for fun." I thought to myself as I ran behind Naomi.

Naomi was always faster than I was, and taller too; I think her height helped her. It rather made me jealous but I would never tell her that.

"Come on Yeshai, you're falling behind!" Naomi called out from the front.

"I'm coming, first one to the town water well gets first portions at dinner tonight!" I competitively countered.

They ran all the way from the fields to the town's square, of course Naomi made it first.

Even the wisest and most powerful individuals can benefit from good council.
   -Prophet

Chapter 5:

Naomi & I

I t was early afternoon and the sun was placed high in the sky as if it was being suspended by an invisible string. The sound of the people conversing and exchanging goods at the town's center could be heard all the way from the fields.

"I told you that I would win, I always win!" Naomi bragged dancing in front of the water well.

Out of breath, Yeshai follows closely behind her, disappointed he kicks the dirt.

"Yea so what, I'm getting better. I will bet you next time!" I snapped in an attempt to preserve what little pride I could.

Naomi just looked at me and smiled, she was the only person I would allow to tease me and get away with it. It was all fun but she always encouraged me to be better as well.

"Yea you did get faster and taller too. I'm sure you will get me next time." She said confidently.

"Well what do you want to do now?" I asked as I leaned over the edge of the water well.

"Hey let's walk by the market, I'm sure we will find something to get into." She said pushing my back as if she wanted to push me over the side.

"Hey that's not funny Naomi!" I scolded holding on for dear life.

She just laughed, but that was Naomi always finding the most efficient ways to get under my skin. We began to walk towards the market; passing by the buildings and watching the adults go about their day.

"It would be great if you guys could move here, then we could play together every day." She smiled and placed her hand on my shoulder.

"Playing every day would be amazing; there aren't many kids out where we live." I eagerly answered.

"Wait that would mean I would have to see your face every day. Hmm never mind its cool with you just visiting from time to time ha." She cleverly insulted me.

She baited me in and I fell right for it.

"Let's see how funny you are when I never come back with father to visit." I muttered aloud while sulking.

I could see the expression on her face begin to change. My pride began to bolster, my chest inflated, and my shoulders rose. Then I saw her expression shift from a state of confusion to confidence and my stomach dropped to the floor.

"Oh no, I thought I had her finally. What is she thinking and what is she about to say!?" I thought as I braced myself for her counter.

She stopped walking and put her hands on her hips similar to her mother.

"Nice try, but you know you could not last out there with no children to play with for long. And you love your Grandmother entirely too much not come to visit!" She boldly retorted.

Immediately I felt the sharp pain from her knife pierce my heart; I died inside.

"Whatever!" I stuttered moving her away from me.

"Aw don't be like that; come on there's the man that sells pigeons!" She quickly changed the subject.

Naomi walked right up to the man as if she dealt business in the market every day.

"How much for a pigeon sir?" Naomi politely asked.

"A half a shekel." The man replied.

"Great I have that much, may I have one please?" She asked.

"Sure my dear, enjoy and may God bless you and your family." He said handing over the pigeon.

"Thank you sir, God bless you and yours as well." She responded after handing him the money and walking back over to me.

"So what are you going to do with that pigeon?" I asked with a confusing look on my face.

"Because it was fun." She replied plainly with a smirk on her face as she tied a small piece of string to the bird's leg.

She let go of the bird and as it tried to fly away, she would pull it back with the string. As we walked, we saw some of the other kids coming our way.

"Naomi what are you guys up to?" The small boy asked as he approached us.

"Hey Naomi, is that Yeshai?" Another boy added.

"Hey guys, we are just hanging out, and yes that's Yeshai." Naomi answered as she softly petted the bird.

I looked at one of the boys closely I could almost recognize him.

"Malakai is that you?" I asked.

"Yea man it's me, how have you been?" He answered reaching out to hug me.

"Wow, it's been a long time since we played together, I thought you moved to Tiberius." I told him.

"Yes we did, but we moved back a few months ago because father got a cool job as a tax collector." He boasted.

"Abijah, what were you and Malakai doing?" Naomi asked.

"We were trying to find something to do, how did you get a bird?" Abijah responded.

"She bought it with her own money." I confidently interjected.

Naomi quickly looked over at me and smiled, then pointed over to this large stack of hay that sat in a wagon.

"Look guys, there's a wagon of hay!" She exclaimed and ran over to it.

"What are we going to do with a wagon of hay?" Abijah and Malakai asked.

I knew Naomi well; she was always trying to do the most daring thing she could think of. She was thinking of somehow finding a way to jump into the wagon of hay.

"Here she goes." I thought to myself.

Naomi gave the pigeon to Abijah and then climbed up the side of one of the buildings using a small stack of crates that sat next to it. Once she reached the top of the building, she crossed over the wooden walkway the bridged between the two buildings.

"We can jump down into the wagon from here!" He shouted as she waved down to us.

"You are out of your mind!" Malakai shouted back.

I began climbing the small crates onto the next ledge leading to the rooftop of the building. Once I reached the top of the building I crossed over on the wooden walkway, the wood creaked like the old chair back at Grandmothers house.

"That a boy Yeshai, I knew you had it in you. Are you ready?" She encouraged.

"Uh um, yea sure." I said stepping back off the ledge as my stomach began to drop.

Naomi smiled and then jumped off the ledge and landed gracefully into the pile of hay. She laid there submerged for moment and then popped up and exploded full of laughter.

"That was so fun; you guys have to try it. Come on Yeshai you can do it!" She called out.

I slowly scooted over the edge and looked over at her. She began to clap and root for me; this made me feel less nervous.

"Well here I go." I said to myself as I began to jump off the roof.

Abijah and Malakai looked on in disbelief, I was not known as the most daring person.

"Ahhhhhhhhh!" I screamed on the way down.

I fell down into the pile of the hay, and surprisingly it was very fun. In that split second, all I could think about was climbing back up and doing it again.

"Are you going to try it Abijah." I asked as I climbed out of the wagon next to Naomi.

"Yea I'll give it a try." He responded as he walked over to climb up.

"Whoa Yeshai!

I fell down into the pile of the hay, and surprisingly it was very fun. In that split second, all I could think about was climbing back up and doing it again.

"Are you going to try it Abijah." I asked as I climbed out of the wagon next to Naomi.

"Yea I'll give it a try." He responded as he walked over to climb up.

"Whoa Yeshai! You did great!" She exclaimed giving me a tight hug.

"Na..Naomi...I.....can't....breath." I muttered, as I turned blue in the face.

"Oh, I'm sorry big head." She said letting me go.

By this time Abijah had jumped off the roof and into the hay pile. We then all looked at Malakai in anticipation.

"Don't look at me; no way am I jumping off of that roof. Besides someone has to watch the bird." He cringed.

"Scared are we? Well ok what about you guys?" She asked the rest of us.

"Oh yea!" We screamed.

We all then climbed the house and jumped down into the hay pile repeatedly for hours. We even made faces in the air and jumped in pairs to enhance the experience. The owner of the wagon was on his way back from the market when he saw us.

"Hey you children, get down from there!" The man screamed.

"Oh no guys, there's a man coming this way!" Malakai warned us.

We jumped down into the hay pile and began to run away. We ran through the market with the man in close pursuit. We climbed under tables and jumped over carts trying to put distance between us. Soon we split up, Naomi, I went one way, and the people went the other way. After a while we noticed we were no longer being chased we stopped to rest.

"Did we get away?" I said hunched over while gasping for air.

"I think so, I don't see him anymore." Naomi replied while also gasping for air.

"What about Malakai and Abijah, do you think they made it?" I asked with concern.

"Well Abijah lives very close to here so I'm sure he ran home and since he is almost as fast as me I don't think the man caught him. As for Malakai, if he did get caught I'm sure his father can work something out with the man being a tax collector and all." She sharply answered.

"Ok if you say so, I hope they made it." I added as I began to walk up the road.

"Where are you going?" She asked.

"To the temple, we don't have much time before supper." I told her.

"Ok let's go." She answered running behind me.

We walked to the temple conversing, laughing, and catching up over lost time. As we got closer to the temple, I saw a man in a black hooded robe with his face covered staring in our direction.

"Why is he looking at us?" I asked aloud.

"Who, who is looking at us." Naomi asked.

"That man over there in the black robe." I said pointing over in his direction.

Naomi tried looking for him but he was no longer there.

"I don't see a man in black, are you seeing things big head." She teased.

"She couldn't see him, was it that same man from before?" I stopped and thought intensely to myself.

"Yeshai, Yeshai are you ok?" She asked.

"Yes, sorry I just could have sworn I saw someone. It doesn't matter lets go we are almost to the temple." I replied scratching my head.

When we arrived, there was a group of teachers of the law standing on the steps of the synagogue arguing over scripture.

"There is no resurrection!" *One man shouted.*

"You are oblivious to the ways of God!" *Another man shouted back.*

"If there was a resurrection, then what's next, we should forgive our enemies too." *He insulted.*

"You are beyond talking to; this boy probable has more knowledge about the Lord our God than you." *He reputed.*

The Pharisee looked over to me as we began walking up the steps to head into the temple. To prove a point he called me over to the group.

"Boy, this man here says that you may know more about scripture than I, a teacher of the law. That you may be more knowledgeable in the ways of God than I so listen closely. He says that there is a resurrection, and that we must forgive our enemies. What do you say?" *He inquired chuckling and folding his arms.*

"Leave the boy alone." *One of the other men from the crowd called out.*

"It's alright young one; you do not have to answer the question." *The Pharisee defending the resurrection assured.*

"Rabbi, but I am just a small boy. Would you really take such heed to my words?" I asked respectfully.

"If you are right, we will all take heed. Now quiet everyone let the boy speak." The Pharisee antagonizing the resurrection added.

Suddenly I felt lightness in my stomach, similar to that feeling I had while jumping off the roof earlier. My head began to pound, but there was no pain and felt this confidence. I walked into the middle of the crown, stood on a small stool, and began to speak to them while Naomi just watched.

"Surely as the Lord lives there will be a resurrection, even Daniel spoke about such things. He said; and many of them that sleep in the dust of the earth shall awake, some to everlasting life, and some to shame and everlasting contempt." I told them with authority.

The men stood there quiet for a moment and then began looking at each other. The Pharisee against the resurrection took a step back and cleared his throat.

"Surely you do not believe this mere child, what can he tell us about God?" *He exclaimed.*

"Rabbi, in regard to forgiving one's enemies, should we not forgive them? Should we not show compassion? My father taught me to love everyone. Just on yesterday, a man with a sword tried to rob us and take all of our belongings. Did we not forgive him and show him kindness instead of wrath and vengeance? As surely as the Lord lives we forgave that man and he turned from his wicked ways and paid reverence to the God of Abraham." I continued as I made gestures with my hands moving through the inside of the crowd.

Some of the men began to nod in agreement, this angered the frustrated Pharisee.

"Forgiveness to someone who would do you harms and plunder everything you and your father owned. Surely you must have done something?" He asked out of frustration.

"Yes of course we did, we helped him fix his broken wagon so he could be on his way." I responded signaling for Naomi to come over to me.

"A very wise answer from such a young boy, we did not expect to hear such wisdom on this day. What is your name?" The Pharisee supporting the resurrection stepped forward and said.

"Yeshai rabbi." I answered respectfully.

"Yeshai, hmm where do I know you from? Who is your father?" He asked.

"I am the son of the carpenter Jesus, the Grandson of Mary." I told him.

"Ah yes, Jesus! I am sure he is very proud to have such an insightful son. There you have it, let us leave from here for it is almost dinner time." The man told the crowd.

"This is blasphemy! Argh!" The other Pharisee rumbled as he stormed down the steps of the temple.

"It is almost dinner time Naomi, let's go." I instructed her.

Naomi nodded in agreement and we began heading down the steps. Once we reached the corner, I looked down the alleyway and saw the angry Pharisee walking away. He stopped and turned around to look at me, gave a sinister smile and then pulled his hood over his face. Suddenly his once grey robe turned in to a dark smoked black, it was the hooded man from before!

"Naomi looks! He was the man I saw early." I shouted.

Naomi looked down the alley but the man was gone.

"Are you ok Yeshai, you seem to be seeing things." She asked.

"He was just there, don't you believe me?" I pleaded.

"Yea of course I believe you big head. That was some impressive stuff, you said earlier to the elders. Where did all of that come from?" She complimented.

"I do not know exactly, once we got to the temple steps I felt something come over me. The words just seemed to fall out, I didn't feel like I was there speaking alone if that makes any sense." I tried to explain.

"Wow that's crazy, well whatever it was you seemed to make that one elder very mad ha." She laughed as placed her hand on my shoulder.

I couldn't help but think about that man again, how could he just transform like that? What did he want, and where did he come from?

"I need answers!" I said aloud.

"Huh, answers to what?" Naomi asked.

"Uh, oh nothing, come one lets go." I deflected.

Naomi and Yeshai walked all the way to her house.

"Are you eating supper with us?" *Naomi asked.*

"No, not tonight it's getting late and I'm sure father and Grandmother is worried about me, I will see you tomorrow ok." I told her.

"Ok big head, see you tomorrow." She said smiling as she gave me a hug and went into the house.

Yeshai turned around and began walking back to his Grandmother's house thinking about what happened at the temple. Something was going on he could feel it. He wanted to speak to his father about it, off in the distance he could see his Grandmother's house with old Sampson standing out front eating a juicy green apple. The orange tint in the sky began to burn into a dark simmer; soon the sun could no longer be seen on the horizon.

"Hey Sampson." *Yeshai murmured as he walked past the colt and into the house.*

**Untapped wisdom is like an iceberg, there is a chance that underneath the surface lies an enormous amount just waiting to be revealed.**
-Prophet

Chapter 6:

Keys to the Kingdom

*Y*eshai walked into the house and his father and *Grandmother were standing in the kitchen preparing supper. Jesus noticed the expression on his face and walked over to him.*

"Is everything alright?" *Jesus asked supportively.*

"No sir, there are things happening that I cannot explain." *Yeshai explained as his father walked him over to the table.*

"Here have a seat, so what exactly is happening?" he asked me.

I looked into his eyes and in my heart I knew that he knew exactly what was going on with me.

"I believe you know father, please help me!" I urged as I placed my hands on his chest.

"Listen my son, there are things you are not yet ready to know. Not because I do not want you to know them but because the Father has chosen it to be so. I can see the questions stirring around in your head, and you are burdened I your heart. What I can tell you is that what you feel and the things you have seen isn't just your imagination." He explained placing his hand on my head.

"You mean the dark figure, the man, the things I was able to do, all of it was true." I staggered back for a moment.

"Yes." He replied.

"Why are all of these things happening to me?" I asked inquisitively.

"Because you are my son and because you have a calling on your life. That is all I can say for now, more will be revealed in due time but you mustn't tell anyone about these things." He firmly answered giving me a stern look.

"Y....yes father I will not tell anyone. And the man in black?" I asked one last time.

"He cannot harm you, do not worry about such things. I know how you handled the situation at the temple, I am very proud of you son." He reassured me.

"How did you know about the temple?" I asked with shock.

"Because the Father told me." He replied with a smile.

Grandmother stood there attentively listening the entire time, she did not say a word. The expression on her face was partly concerned but she still managed to smile at me.

"Alright my dear boy, it's time to eat." *She interjected as she placed the bowls in front of them and sat down.*

"Yes ma'am, Grandmother Can I ask you a question?" I said looking over at father for approval.

He nodded to me to speak as she began breaking the bread and handing us our portions.

"Yes dear you can ask me anything." He assured me.

"Did you know about all of this?" I asked.

"Somewhat, all that has been revealed to me is that you are a special boy. You were chosen by God to do great things, what happens day-to-day is yet for me to know. If the Father decides I should know more then he will reveal it to me." She said smiling.

Although this moment was awkward, I did not know how to make sense out of it. I mean after all I'm just a child, but it felt good to know that they were talking to me plainly. This was the first time that I felt my speaking direct and not answering my questions with more questions or parables. My entire life I felt different from other children, I was beginning to understand why. Although this day answered some of my major questions, it did not quite put out the fire that burned inside of me. Instead, it did quite the opposite; it burned many more questions in my head.

"Chosen by God to do great things?" I thought quietly to myself as I ate my meal.

Grandmother gave father a look of concern while we sat at the table. I am not sure what she was thinking but whatever it was father resolved it when he placed his hand on her hand and nodded at her. He had a way to calm any storm a person was going through, I remember back when I was very young we came here to visit and a woman was crying in the middle of the street holding her dead husband. He had been ill for some time and must have collapsed as they were walking. Well father walked up to the woman and wiped her tears, and then he whispered something in her ear and walked back over to mother and me. The woman stopped crying, and allowed some men to carry her husband off with a cart.

"Father?" I called out to him while remembering that moment in time.

He looked at me.

"Yes?" He answered.

"What did you whisper to that woman whose husband had died?" I questioned.

"The Father told me to tell her not to cry, and that he saw her pain and would remove it. For her to leave that place and that he will provide for her for the rest of her life." He told me with a smile.

I just stared at him in amazement. To stop the tears of a woman whose husband had just died was beyond my understanding.

"What an amazing God we serve!" I thought to myself.

"Thank you for all of the supplies you brought me Yeshai, may God bless you." Mary said in an attempt to change the subject.

"You're welcome, I love coming to visit you." I answered her.

"How was it seeing Naomi again?" She asked.

"It was fun, Naomi bought a bird, and we played in hay with some of the other children too!" I exclaimed.

"My oh my, it seemed that you had a very eventful day, what will you do tomorrow?" She politely patronized me.

"Your Grandmother says that they need help with repairs to the temple." He told me.

"Oh great! Can Naomi come too?" I asked with excitement.

"Sure just as long as it is alright with her parents, and if she is willing to work." He answered pointing his finger in my direction.

"Yes! Thank you father!" I exclaimed while giving him a very tight hug.

After we ate, we prayed and gave thanks for our food. I began to think of my mother back home and missed her. I wanted her to be able to travel with us; I loved traveling as a family. We once journeyed to this far away city to sell some furniture father made for their temple. Mother and father held each other's hand and sat me a top of Sampson. We had to go through the mountains at one point; I could see the entire land off in the distance. I could see the birds flying past our heads and off into the sunlight. Mother would pick up a random rock, give it to me, and say that I should always cherish seeing new places especially with family.

"Always cherish seeing new places especially with family." I said aloud to myself looking out Grandmother's window.

Yeshai began to smile as he reminisced. Jesus walks up behind him and places his hand on his shoulder.

"I miss her too son." He said reassuringly.

I looked up at him; I could see the pain of being without her in his eyes.

"Come; let's head over to the temple." Father said shaking my head with his hand and then heading over to the door.

We stopped at Naomi's house along the way. I eagerly ran up to their door and knocked, her mother answered.

"Well good morning Yeshai, how are you today?" She nicely asked.

"I'm doing very well ma'am, is Naomi home?" I politely responded signaling over for father to come over.

I knew that seeing that father here with me would increase the chances of Naomi's parents allowing her to come with us.

"Naomi, Yeshai is here to see you. Hello Jesus, it is very good to see you, please come inside." She respectfully insisted.

"I am well, it is very nice to see you as well Susanna." Father replied.

As we walked inside, I saw Naomi's father sitting at the table, when he saw father he stood up to greet him.

"Jesus greetings, how long has it been? God's favor must be upon us this morning, welcome." He said with open arms.

"Aaron, truly God's favor is upon you and your house. It has been too long old friend." Father replied embracing him.

Naomi emerged from the back and we all sat at their table while Susanna began watering the plants.

"So what brings you two buy this morning?" Aaron asked.

"Yeshai and I are headed to the temple to make some repairs. We wanted to know if it was alright if Naomi tagged along." Father explained.

Aaron looked over at Susanna and then looked back over at us with approval.

"Of course she may go with you; maybe she will come back to us a fine carpenter." He boasted jokingly.

"Dad!" Naomi scowled.

We all began to laugh.

"Jesus, you all have a wonderful time over at the temple, this evening why don't you all come over for dinner. It will be nice to catch up and Mary can bring over her delicious wheat bread." Susanna invited.

"Thank you for your hospitality; we would be honored to join you." Father accepted with a smile.

Naomi hugged her parents as we headed outside. Along the way to the temple father began to speak.

"Do you know how important you are to God Naomi?" He asked reaching out his hand to touch the tips of the tall flowers as he walked along.

"Oh no, father is about to go on one of his rants, this is embarrassing." I thought to myself as I let out a soft sigh.

"Um...no." Naomi softly answered.

"It is ok Naomi; many do not know the importance of their lives. For we are God's most favorite creation and because of that we are given favor. For the father is all knowing and all powerful and he has entrusted a lot to us." Father continued.

"Like what?" Naomi seemed to be intrigued.

I looked over at her face and noticed a slight smile and my embarrassment began to fade away.

"She actually is listening to him and enjoying this, wow I'm impressed." I thought to myself once again as I began to clear my throat.

"The keys to the Kingdom of Heaven have already been given to you. It is our responsibility to become aware of it and to make others aware of it as well. If you are locked in a prison cell and it has not been made known to you that you already have the key to get out. You will spend all your time trying to think of solutions without ever checking your pocket for a key. Then a man comes in white and tells you that the key is in your pocket, you will be surprised and then open the cell and get out. But there are many others locked in cells trying to get out, will you then go and tell them that their keys are in their pockets?" He asked her in a parable.

"Yes of course I would, I love helping people. Well at least the good ones, some of them may be criminals and need to stay in their cells." She quickly responded.

"But everyone is considered a criminal to the Father, and yet he still has given us the keys to the Kingdom of Heaven." Jesus told her as he began to look over to me.

I had heard this parable before, but it did not make sense to me until this very moment. My mind had been opened, it is almost as if back when he told me and mothers this he was staging and preparing me for this.

"But why would God give us the keys to the Kingdom of Heaven if we are criminals?" She asked confusingly.

"Now that is the question I was waiting for!" Father exclaimed with a smile.

"Because God loves us just that much." I politely interjected.

"Wow Yeshai how did you know that?" She asked with opened eyes.

"I knew God loved us before, but it wasn't until just now that I had an answer for you." I told her while looking over to father.

He looked back at me and nodded in approval. We noticed that Naomi was blown away at what she had heard.

"So if we are all criminals to God, and he still gives us the Keys to the Kingdom of Heaven. Once I am let out of my cell, I should go and tell everyone else how to get out of his or hers regardless of what they have done because God loves us that much. It almost sounds like I should love them that much in order to tell them about the key in the first place." She said as she attempted to put the pieces together.

"Exactly my child, we are to love one another with God's love in order to make them aware of their key." *Jesus rejoiced.*

"Father, in the story the key is in the person's pocket right?" I asked.

"Yes son." He replied.

"But since we are talking about loving one another as God loves us, shouldn't the Key to the Kingdom of Heaven be in our hearts?" I asked once again with a slight fear of being wrong.

"Absolutely! Truly, I tell you, you children are young in body but are mature in spirit. There will come a time when many adults will have much trouble understanding this. However, you who are young and of little experience can grasp every word spoken here today; surely, the Kingdom of Heaven awaits the two of you. For I know the Father is pleased on this day!" *Jesus exclaimed as he gave thanks to God.*

Father was overjoyed I have not seen him this happy in a long time. Naomi was also smiling as we walked; it felt good to learn new things about God. As I began to smile, I began to feel bad about being embarrassed earlier.

"I should apologize to father." I thought.

"There is no need to for guilt my son, for many will be embarrassed at my words, and even more will be angry at my words. I have already forgiven you before we left Naomi's house." He softly whispered leaning over to me.

"Yeshai your father is a good man; you are blessed to have him." She complimented with a smile.

"Thank you Naomi, I think so too." I said jokingly while nudging father.

"Oh you think so huh, hmmm well I think that you are a good son too then." Father replied jokingly as he nudged me back.

Naomi just looked at us and laughed.

"Never have I seen such a pair of father and son as you two." She continued laughing.

We continued walking and the temple began to come into view. We passed the merchant who sold Naomi the bird as well as the wagon of hay from the day before. Once we reached the temple one of the men from yesterday came over to greet us. He was the teacher of the law that had pleaded the case for the resurrection and that had spoken to me afterwards.

"Greetings! Welcome to the temple, you are just in time." The man said with open arms.

"Thank you sir, we are here to do some repairs." Father answered.

"Yes sir, it is very nice to see you Jesus. It has been too long, and who do we have here?" He said looking down at Naomi.

"My name is Naomi sir; I am here to help too." She announced.

"Oh my, well I am sure grateful to have you here Naomi, my name is Hadad and it's very nice to meet you. Moreover, Yeshai, it is very nice to see you again, you are a very special young man. Jesus this one here is truly a gift from God, I'm not sure if you are unaware of what took place here yesterday but he was amazing!" Hadad complimented.

"Yes I am aware of what took place here yesterday, and I am very proud of him as well. Every day he shows me new things and surprises me, just today on the way over here they both said some things pleasing to the Lord's ears." Father agreed.

"Oh really, well you must tell me the story sometime, I would love to hear it." He replied.

"Soon, but first please show us where the repairs need to be made." Father answered.

"Certainly, follow me this way." He said guiding us into the temple.

We walked inside the courtyard and there were women praising God. There were also different rooms off in each corner of the courtyard. As we continued, we entered yet another gate that opened into another courtyard. There were priests walking about and offering tables where the animals were to be slaughtered there. As we continued, we walked some steps and went through these large doors. Ahead of us was a large room with a large red curtain draped down over the entrance of the room. To the left and right was smaller rooms or halls, but Hadad had taken us into this room directly to the right of the entrance door.

"Here is where the repairs need to be made, this room has a dreadful leak, and every time it rains water covers the floor. You come highly recommended so I'm sure you are more than capable of handling the situation." Hadad said pointing to the hole in the ceiling.

"Yes Lord willing, I was told that the tools and supplies would be provided." Father answered.

"Oh yes of course, there is a ladder over there next to the table and all the supplies you'll require are already on the roof. The carpenter that came a few weeks ago could not get the job done." He mentioned as he left the room.

"Very well, let us begin." Father instructed.

Jesus and the two children prepared to begin the repairs to the roof of the room right outside the sanctuary.

Only those truly without sight are blind, such handicaps are not in regards to the eyes but instead to the hearts and minds of man.
-Prophet

Chapter 7:

A Carpenter's Hands

Y eshai can you place the ladder just over there because I want to see the extent of the damage?" Father asked pointing over in the direction of the spot on the floor underneath the hole.

"What would you like me to do?" Naomi asked politely.

"So eager to help, I am pleased. Very well, I hear that you are quite the climber; you can climb up and tell me what you see." Jesus said encouragingly.

"Ok!" Naomi replied smiling revealing much excitement.

I placed the ladder firm in the place father directed and Naomi wasted little time climbing to the top.

"What do you see my dear?" Father asked.

"I can see the entire courtyard from here!" She exclaimed.

"Yes it's beautiful I'm sure, but what about the roof; what do you see?" He continued with a laugh.

"Oh I'm sorry yes, I see broken pieces spread out over the roof and the wood is very wet." Naomi replied attempting to replace her enthusiasm with professionalism.

"Very good Naomi, are the pieces that are broken square shaped or rectangle shaped?" Father asked attempting to gain evaluating information.

"They are square, but there are a few long rectangular shaped pieces up here as well." She answered.

"It seems the roof was poorly constructed which led to corrosion of the top level of panels due to the heavy rain. The water must have seeped through easily enough to corrode the lower level of supporting panels. We will have to replace the support panels first and then move on to the top-level panels last. Father explained to me.

"You will need someone on the roof if that is the case right father?" I asked attempting to understand the situation.

"Yes, you and Naomi will sit atop the roof and pass me the supplies needed to rebuild the lower level. Then once that is complete, you two can start on the top level and I will supervise. You are familiar with how to handle the tools so you can teach Naomi the basics and I'll help when needed." Father confidently instructed.

He always encouraged me to teach and lead when it came to others. That was his way, he would show me how to do different things and then let me go and show someone else what I learned. It felt good teaching someone else; I think it made me better especially when it came to carpentry.

"Naomi goes ahead and climbs on top of the roof and I'll climb up behind you." I instructed her.

Naomi climbed up to the roof and Yeshai follow close behind. As Jesus began repairing the lower level Yeshai was explaining the process to Naomi in great detail. He told her how to use the various tools, and what to do and what not to do in certain situations. After he explained what needed to happen, he let her try and she caught on rather quickly. After a few hours, the lower level was nearly completed.

"The rest of the repairs to the lower level can be done from up there; I will head around with the ladder and meet you all shortly." Father said as he began climbing down.

We sat there on the roof looking off into the vast distance. We could see the rest of the temple as the people came and went. We could also see the rest of the town even the mountains to the east. I wondered about home and the thoughts of mother and how she was doing raced across my mind as I let out a soft sigh.

"What's the matter big head?" Naomi teased.

"I just miss my mother." I softly answered with my head tilted downward.

"I'm sure she misses you too, you will see her again soon. I bet she is very proud of you with how much you know about this stuff." She said in an attempt to cheer me up.

"What stuff?" I asked confused.

"This stuff with your father, using tools and building things. It is very cool I wish I could do this stuff like you two." She added.

"Oh yea, it's alright I guess. It was hard at first but once you get used to it, it gets easier." I replied.

"It must have taken a lot of time huh?" She asked.

"Yea, father has been teaching me things since I can remember." I answered her, my voice began to pick up.

"Wow that is amazing, hey thanks again for letting me tag along I have had a really fun time today." She continued as she placed her hand on my shoulder.

"It is no problem at all, I had fun too." I answered.

After a few minutes of talking, father came up to us from the side facing the main courtyard and sat next to us.

"Beautiful isn't it, God's creation." He stated staring up into the sky.

"Yea it is, it must have taken a lot to make." Naomi said placing her hand over her eyes to shield them from the sunlight.

"Oh yes. Let us finish the roof, son could you hand me the hammer?" Father replied.

I handed the hammer to father while Naomi handed him the nails. Once he had the lower foundation in place, he let us finish it. Before we knew it, a few hours had gone by and the roof was completed.

"Wow, I didn't think we would finish up that fast." I said taking Naomi by the hand to help her to her feet.

"Yea, time just seemed to fly by. I was having so much fun just working." She added with a smile.

After heading down the ladder, Jesus and the children were met by high priest on their way into the courtyard.

"Finished for the day, coming back tomorrow to finish up I see?" The high priest asked.

"No sir, we have finished all of the repairs." Jesus replied.

"All of the repairs!? Why that hole in the roof was big enough for me to climb through." He exclaimed in shock.

"Yes it was a large hole indeed, but I came with help and these too really make a difference. Is there anything else you need repaired?" Jesus said placing each hand on their heads.

"Um no, no that was all that needed repairing. Nevertheless, thank you very much for your hard work. Please accept these denarii as a token of the temple's appreciation." The high priest offered reaching out a hand full of gold coins.

"Oh no we did not work for pay, but that God may bless you and all who come to the temple." Jesus refused.

"But I insist, surely you all could use this. Worry not for we have plenty." He persistently explained.

"If you have plenty, why not give to the poor, the orphan, or widow? We say that we did not work for pay, take your money, and bless someone else just as God has blessed you." Jesus told him.

The high priest's face began to turn; you could see aggravation begin to build.

"Who are you to instruct me on what to do with the temple funds? I am the high priest here and I demand respect!" he yelled.

"Have I shown you any disrespect? If so, please tell me how? Even prophets and kings are subject to God, and should be obedient to his word. A high priest is no different; if you begin to give willingly those who follow you will give also." Jesus humbly explained.

Naomi and I watched closely, we saw the man stand there quietly for a moment. It looked as if he wanted to say something in response but for some reason he could not find the words. This seemed to make him even more upset.

"Thank you all for repairing the roof, you may take your leave now." The high priest grumbled turning away and heading inside the inner court.

We then began our journey back home.

"Why was that man so upset?" Naomi asked as we walked.

"Sometimes men do not like to be corrected, especially from someone they consider of less standing." Father explained.

"He was the high priest right?" I asked looking up at father.

"Yes he was." Father replied.

"I have never seen anyone talk to a high priest like that before." Naomi added in awe.

"Many are afraid of the truth, never be afraid to speak on God's word. Even if it may upset the one you are talking to." Jesus explained further.

"I can see why you are so wise Yeshai, you get it from your father." Naomi complimented.

"Thank you." I said with a smile.

"Yes Yeshai has a bright future ahead of him, and so do you Naomi." Father told both of us.

We continued walking and finally arrived at Naomi's house. The sun began to set over the horizon, as the cloud seemed to dissipate into the clear darkening sky.

"Thank you for taking me with you today. I will see you all tonight for dinner right?" Naomi shouted as she waved over to us.

"Of course we will, Lord willing." Father answered waiving back.

We entered the house and grandmother was already preparing bread for supper.

"Mother, we have been invited over to Aaron and Susanna's for dinner." Jesus told her.

"Oh my! That would be great let me gather what I've prepared so far." Mary said excitingly as she wrapped up the cooked bread in a cloth towel.

"Yeshai go and clean yourself, for we will be leaving shortly for dinner." Jesus told him.

"Yes father." I replied heading to the back.

After the remaining bread, Grandmother prepared was finished and we were all ready for supper we headed over to their home.

As we approached the door, Aaron had already been standing there waiting with open arms.

"Welcome friends! Come inside." He invited.

As we entered Grandmother and Naomi's mother embraced. Father and Naomi's father sat down and began to talk.

"It is so nice to come over and have dinner Susanna, thank you for your hospitality." Mary told her.

"Oh it is no trouble at all, thank you for coming and bringing your magnificent bread with you. Oh how I love it!" Susanna replied with her mouthwatering as she placed the bread on the table.

Naomi came over and gave me a hug, then began helping the women set the table. I must admit seeing everyone talking and enjoying himself or herself made being away from mother slightly more tolerable. Everyone here has always treated each other like family. As I sat next to father I looked across the room at Naomi and something seemed different about her for a moment. Her gentile green eyes and soft smile hiding behind her long black hair.

"What was this feeling?" I asked myself before shaking my head.

"Dinner is almost ready everyone." Susanna announced.

"Good, my stomach was beginning to rumble." Aaron boasted.

"It has been so nice to cook with you Susanna; we must do this again sometime." Mary told her.

"Oh yes, we must do this again." She replied.

"Jesus you are quiet tonight, is everything ok?" Aaron asked placing his hand on Jesus's shoulder.

"Oh yes, I am just enjoying this time with family. Your daughter has shown much promise with carpentry." Jesus answered leading Aaron over to Naomi with his eyes.

"Really is that so, hmm I suppose that doesn't surprise me seeing that she loves doing physical things." Aaron acknowledged with a smile.

"Oh, did you at least enjoy yourself dear?" Mary asked Naomi.

"Yes ma'am, I learned a lot today." Naomi politely responded.

"Pretty soon there will be repairs needed around here; I'm glad that our daughter is a fine carpenter then." Susanna teased.

Everyone began to laugh while Naomi scowled with her arms folded. We then sat down and began eating dinner and share stories about how life has been since we last came here to Nazareth. We gave thanks for our food and thanked God for his provision and many blessings.

"This was a very good night. When will you be heading back home Jesus?" Aaron asked.

"Tomorrow morning." Father replied.

"Well you must come again soon, we miss your company and do bring Sabella with you next time it has been too long." Susanna said wiping the few breadcrumbs from her face.

"We will come back soon once the house is finished, and Sabella will join us." Jesus answered.

"Ok see you later big head, I had fun!" Naomi teased giving me another hug.

We said our goodbyes and headed back to Grandmother's. I was excited about going home but I knew I would miss Naomi. I had not thought of my wooden toy horse all day.

The hands of man can mend a broken object and create them, but the hands of God can mend a broken heart and create beautiful memories.
-Prophet

Chapter 8:

Purgatory

The star's light sparkled in the sky like a glimmer of glass that ripped across a calm body of water. The moon was full giving of a vivid glow that with the addition of starlight gave the night a sense of aura. The streets were quiet; all that could be heard were the echoes of animal sounds off in the distance.

As I lay there staring at the ceiling I wondered about the view from the roof of the temple. To be able to sit there and watch the people travel to and from and the birds fly across the sky was amazing. Tomorrow we will be traveling back home, I thought about everything that had happened the past few days. Especially the conversation with Grandma Mary and father back at her house. And how was I able to speak about the word of God to the elders that way back at the temple? All these questions raced across my mind like the rushing waters of the Nile, and then slowly everything went dark. When I awoke, it was quiet and greys as if a group of clouds were blocking the sun. Father was nowhere to be found, and the smell of burning wood was in the air. It was strong; I almost had to cover my face to refrain from coughing. As I stood to my feet, I could see fires off in the distance, the flames stood taller than the surrounding trees.

"What is going on? And where is father?" I asked myself as I looked around for any sign that he was near.

I was no longer at Grandmother's house but in an open field on the outskirts of the village. I could hear screams echoing from the village, I had a bad feeling about it but something was drawing to head in that direction. As I got closer there was a crying woman holding her child in her arms.

"Oh my baby, my sweet sweet baby, why?" The woman cried out holding her daughters head tightly against her breast.

When she saw me, her eyes filled with rage.

"It was you; you did this to my child!" She exclaimed pointing her finger judgmentally at me.

I was confused, for I had never seen the woman before in my life.

"How could I do this?" I thought as I cautiously continued to approach.

The woman's posture began to get aggressive as she began to scream and call for help.

"Ma'am I do not know what you speak of, why do you accuse me of causing harm to you? For I have never seen you or your daughter in all my days. How could I do such a thing?" I asked as I attempted to make sense of all of this.

"No, you know of which I speak. You did this to my child, you did all of this! Look at all the damage you have caused, you cannot fool me. Now stay back!" She screamed as her eyes filled with tears and her nose ran loosely.

"I'm sorry for your loss, but I assure you that I had no part of this." I replied defensively.

"I saw you! You came from the hills on a black horse and you wore a black hood. You caused the sky to darken and you began attacking the people. My daughter and I managed to make it out of the village only to be met here by you. You killed my daughter, and now you are here to finish your work to kill me also!" She accused.

Her voice was very confident; I could tell she truly believed I was responsible for all of this. However, when did I do this? A black horse? A black hood? This did not make sense at all.

"I am not here to harm you, you have my word." I assured her placing my hands in the air while still approaching her cautiously.

Once I got a few feet from her she stood to her feet and picked up a large branch off the ground in an attempt to defend herself.

"Wait, your eyes, there is something different about your eyes." She paused.

"My eyes, what about my eyes?" I asked her.

"They were black as night, and had no life in them. But your eyes are warm, gently, like my daughters." She explained as she slowly began to lower the branch.

"I wish I knew what was going on here, my eyes have always been like this." I attempted to explain reaching out my hand for the branch.

"I can see that you are not the monster that did all of this, but it looked just like you." She said placing the large branch on the floor.

Ashes from the flames began to fall to the ground like tainted snowflakes.

"Thank you for believing me, I know you are in no position to do so and I really am sorry for your lost. But I am looking for my father, have you seen anyone come this way?" I asked sympathetically.

"No, I have not. You are the only one to pass this way." She answered as she kneeled down over her daughter.

I looked down at her daughter laying there lifeless as the small pieces of ash gently began to cover her face. Suddenly I heard a familiar voice call out to me.

"Yeshai, speak to her." The voice faintly instructed.

"Speak to her? What am I to say?" I asked.

The woman looked confused as to why Yeshai was talking to himself.

"Speak to her." The voice whispered again.

Yeshai turned towards the woman, following the voice's instruction.

"What is your name?" He asked holding his head trying to make sure he was not going crazy.

"Ishmael, my name is Ishmael." She reluctantly answered.

"No, speak to the child." The mysterious voice echoed once more, this time more persistent than the previous times.

"How am I to speak to the child, she is dead." I unknowingly said aloud.

"What are you saying? Are you trying to insult me!?" Ishmael asked angrily.

"I am hearing this voice, it's telling me to speak to your daughter. I do not know what it means by speak to her since she is gone, can you hear it?" I tried to explain.

"No I have not heard any voice, who are you?" She answered in confusion looking back and forth between her daughter and me.

I walked over, crouched next to her daughter, and glanced up to Ishmael for her approval. She reluctantly nodded as I turned back to her daughter, instantly I knew exactly what to say to her.

"By the power of God you shall live, rise!" I declared as I touched her forehead.

Immediately I felt a surge of power build up in me, I could feel it in my belly and then in the hand in which I used to touch her forehead. The girl opened her eyes and let out a loud gasp for air as if she had been holding her breath the entire time.

"My God! How did you!? Baby, my baby!" Ishmael hysterically shouted snatching her daughter in her arms and holding her close.

I stood back in awe laying witness to the reunion.

"What just happened? What did I just do?" I thought to myself.

"Mom? Mom is that you?" The girl asked in a raspy voice like the one she had just awoke from a deep sleep.

"Yes it's me my love, I'm here." She replied with tears flowing uncontrollably.

"Where am I? What happened to me?" The girl asked confusingly as she began to stand to her feet.

Her clothes were still stained with blood from her now healed wounds. As she turned to me, she jumped back in fear.

"Mom it's him, it's the one who came and hurt all those people!" She exclaimed.

"No my dear, it is not he. This young man saved your life, you lay there lifeless in my arms, and he brought you back to me. Look into his eyes, his eyes will tell you that he is not the one behind all of this. She quickly interjected in an attempt to clear my name.

The girl stared at me intensely glancing up and down as if I were being examined by a healer.

"Yes you are right in saying this one isn't the monster with the black hood. His eyes are different." She concluded.

"My name is Yeshai it is very nice to meet you." I introduced myself in an attempt to quench the tension of the situation.

"Thank you Yeshai for saving my daughter, for God works through you." Ishmael earnestly told him.

"Yes thank you also, I am Rachel." The girl added.

"And you as well Rachel, but I have to find my father and something is telling to go down to the village. You two should get as far away from this place as you can." I implored pointing into the opposite direction as the chaos.

"True the danger seems to be in that direction but we have laid witness to God's power first hand through you. You seem like the safest option so we will come with you." Ishmael explained.

"For I cannot protect either of you, I am just a boy." I said in an attempt to sway them to leave.

"Just a boy, did you not just give life to the lifeless? We are coming with you!" She insisted.

Seeing that there was no way for me changing her mind I decided to let them come along with me to the village.

"Very well, you can accompany me to the village but if anything happens promise me that you will run and not look back.

"Yes we will do that." They agreed.

"Now can you tell me more about what happened here?" I asked as we began walking the direction of the town.

One could still smell the burnt air festering as the fires continued to flicker off in the distance. Yeshai and the girls headed down towards the village and came upon a small shack right off the road. As they approached it the front door slowly creaked open.

"Look!" Rachel screamed.

A man emerged from the dark inside the hut, he face free of emotion and foam slightly lingered on the corner of his mouth.

"Are you ok?" I asked calling out as we began to walk towards him.

The man just gave a sinister smile and began to laugh.

"He is demon possessed." The voice warned him.

"Demon possessed?" I asked the voice.

The man was slouched over as if he was carrying something on his back, his clothes were tattered, and he had nothing on his feet. Ishmael and Rachel stood in fear as the man began to step closer.

"We are one, we are many, come to play (Then he began speaking in an unknown tongue in a different voice.)" the man screeched.

"What do you want with us?" I asked as fear began to fester in my bones.

"We know you, we are here to serve." The demon-possessed man answered, this tie in a different demonic voice than before.

"How do you know me, and serve who?" I asked once again taking a few steps back.

"Yes we know you; you are the bringer of death and darkness. It is by your hand that we have come, and by your hand the hearts of man will tremble!" The man explained as he charged forward at them.

"Get back you two; this man has a demon inside of him!" I exclaimed placing myself in front of them.

When the man reached them, he attempted to snatch Rachel from Ishmael's arms. Yeshai reacting in the only way the fear would allow in that moment reached out to attempt to pry the man's hands away from Rachel.

"Ah, let go of her!" Ishmael yelled attempting to hold on to Rachel.

As Yeshai's hand came into contact with the man's arm it seared it intensely causing him to scream and let go of Rachel.

"Argh, you hurt us! We will see you again!" The man screamed as he let go of Rachel and ran off into the darkness holding his arm.

Rachel and Ismael feel to the floor in tears holding one another.

"Are you okay?" I gently asked them while trying to regain my breath.

"Yes we are not harmed. But that man, he said he knew you, he said that (THEY) knew you." Ishmael interrogated.

"Yes but I do not know why or how, maybe it has something to do with the one you said looks like me with the black hood." I answered trying to make sense of it all.

At that moment, I knew I had to continue on to the village even more so now.

"Maybe father is there with Grandma Mary and Naomi." I thought to myself while helping them to their feet.

I looked at the two of them as we began walking towards the village.

"You don't have to come with me you know? You can flee back into the hills and find somewhere safe." I attempted to persuade them.

"Nowhere is safe, they are things like him all over the place. Where would we go? No the safest place is with you!" Ishmael exclaimed.

Rachel was so scared that she even held my hand as we walked. Her grip was tight, so tight in fact that her hand was shaking as her fingers wrapped themselves around mine. The smell of burning wood became stronger as we approached Nazareth, there were people running in a panic. I could not image something this bad ever happening, the screams of the people with all this destruction was too much to contend with.

Yeshai looked upon the faces of the lifeless bodies that lay in the street and became sick to his stomach. No child his age should lay witness so such things; in fact, no man should lay witness to such things. The day became cold; the grey overcast began to darken as the sun began to hide itself behind the horizon. Yeshai, Ishmael, and Rachel found themselves in the middle of darkness. The only light that managed to pierce through was the burning flames, homes, farms, and even what seemed to be like a section of the temple was burning. In a panic people attacked each other, if felt as though there was no presence of God. Such chaos could only be described as purgatory.

The absence of God in one's heart welcomes the presence of evil.
-Prophet

Chapter 9:

A Sweet Summer's Night

*D*arkness covered the entire area; small pockets of light from the fames could be seen. The sky was black, even the moon had a strange dullness to it as if its light could not reach the ground. The group stayed closely together as they headed for Mary's house. When they arrived, the door was clinging by a single bolt to the hinge swaying back and forth in the eerie breeze. Yeshai ran inside hoping to find his father and Grandmother but no one was there. Everything was a mess, the furniture was overturned, and there were splattered bloodstains against one of the walls. Yeshai began to get extremely worried for his family and tears began to build in his eyes. Rachel and Ishmael followed him inside and when they saw him in tears they attempted to comfort him.

"There now little one, I'm sure your family is fine." *Ishmael said placing her hand on his head.*

"Yea there are probable somewhere safe and sound." *Rachel added following her mother's lead.*

Yeshai looked up at them and could recognize the effort but could not help but feeling lost, scared, and slightly responsible all at once.

"Thank you, you two are very kind. But I'm not sure where my family is." *He interjected.*

"Maybe they are out looking for you as well." *Rachel told him pointing back outside the door.*

"Yes maybe you're right, but where would they look for me if not here?" *Yeshai asked.*

"Um, I'm not quite sure but it would probably be a place that you have visited before." *Ishmael answered placing her hand on her chin in deep thought.*

"Hmmm, a place we have visited before? Wait, I know where they may be, it has to be the temple!" *Yeshai exclaimed jumping up in a burst of energy.*

I grabbed their hands and ran for the door as fast as I could; there was a lot of ground to cover to get to the temple.

"Oh dear, wait Yeshai." Ishmael shouted as she and Rachel were being pulled outside and down the road.

They traveled up the road cautiously, avoiding any danger along the way. They hid underneath wagons, in between the buildings, and even inside large water jars to refrain from being seen. As they walked, Yeshai noticed the small merchant tent where Naomi bought the small bird. It had caught fire and the merchant laid there with a farmer's tool embedded in his back dead. Once they arrived at the temple here was a group of demon-possessed men standing in front of the gate. The man whom Yeshai burned with his touch led them.

"It seems we have met again, as I told you we would." *The man cringed in yet another voice, still holding his arm.*

Yeshai looked helplessly into the crowd of demon-possessed individuals. Their eyes were as back as the night sky, and their hands were covered in blood.

"How will be get to the temple?" *Rachael asked still clinging to both of their arms.*

"You wish to enter the temple? My Lord we will not harm you, he is waiting." *One of the demon possessed men explained as his voice shifted from different pitches.*

"I do not trust you; I don't trust any of you." *Yeshai exclaimed.*

"If we wanted you harmed would we not have done so already? Give any command and we shall obey." *The seared man replied.*

"If this is true stand aside and grant us passage into the temple." *Yeshai ordered.*

The demons did as Yeshai commanded and dispersed to either side of the entrance leaving a clear passage through to the temple. Reluctant to enter, the group slowly walked passed the men and entered the temple courtyard. Once inside the men regrouped at the entrance cutting off the exit, Yeshai and the girls continued to push forward inside the temple. There was no one inside the temple and no sign of his father, Grandmother, or Naomi.

"No one is here..." *Yeshai slowly acknowledged as he slouched down onto a bench that sat up against the wall.*

Rachel and her mother sat next to him, shortly afterwards the sound of footsteps echoed from the hall. Yeshai stood up to see who was coming, and it was the young man with the black hood. Ishmael instantly felt cold in fear, as if her very spirit had left her body right there next to her daughter as she looked at him.

"He is the one who killed Rachel!" *Ishmael exclaimed still unable to move.*

As the young man in the hood approached, the lights from the small flames were extinguished as he passed them. The room became dark, the only light visible was from some flames that were on the ceiling on the other side of the room.

"What are you?" *Yeshai asked squinting his eyes trying to see who the man was.*

"I am you, and yet I am no one at all." *The man suspiciously answered.*

"Where is my family?" *Yeshai demanded.*

"They are not here; I brought you to this place to show you the amazing things we can accomplish together. All of this can be done by your hand; it's too bad they had to die to ensure you accept your destiny." *The hooded young man explained as he slowly paced back and forth.*

"Die?" *Yeshai asked as he turned around. Both Rachel and Ismael were dead sitting against the wall on the bench with their throats slashed.*

"What have you done?" *Yeshai shouted running over to them to tend to their wounds but it was too late.*

"You are wise for your age but there is still so much you know nothing about, come with me and I will never hide anything from you. I know you have questions, and I shall answer them. I will not shield you from the truth, and you will know me and I you." *The hooded man continued.*

"I do not want anything from you, I just want my father." *Yeshai answered as tears began to build up once more.*

"Your father can't save you; he can't even tell you the full truth about who he is. Aren't you ready to know who you are instead of being handed confusing parables, to be spoken to plainly?" *The man persuaded.*

Yeshai began to get slightly intrigued by his words.

"What is this truth regarding my father?" I asked sharply.

"Ask him who he is, but first you must do one thing." *The man sinisterly instructed.*

"And what is that?" *Yeshai asked.*

The man then walked up to Yeshai and turned into the dark shadowy figure Yeshai had seen before the few times before.

"You must wake up." *He said slowly as everything turned black.*

"Wake up, Yeshai, son wake up!" *A familiar voice called out.*

Yeshai opened his eyes to immense sunlight, once his sight adjusted to the surroundings his focus came into to view. It was his father calling him.

"Wake up son; you have been sleeping all morning. We have to prepare for the journey back home." *Jesus told him firmly rubbing the top of his head.*

Realizing that was he had experienced was a dream he became bewildered. He slowly stood to his feet and let out a huge stretch. Immediately a sense of relief covered him, for he saw his father and Grandmother safe and healthy. After breakfast they packed Sampson and began heading back, Naomi was with her mother in the fields.

"Yeshai! Hey over here!" *Naomi shouted over to them from the other side of the field as they walked by.*

"Look, there is Naomi Yeshai." Father signaled to me as he tapped me on the arm.

"Hello Naomi!" I shouted in return with a smile.

It felt like I had not seen Naomi is some time due to the very vivid dream. So seeing her face as she ran towards me was warm, and reassuring.

"Are you going back home?" She asked.

"Yea, I have to get away from you." I teased with a chuckle.

"Oh is that right, I know you will miss me big head. I'm the only thing giving that wooden horse of yours a break ha ha." She teased back as I gave her a scowl.

We talked for a few minutes while father spoke to her mother then we said our goodbyes and headed back on the journey home. As we walked father seemed to be in good spirits, he hummed songs and danced as he walked.

"Father, what has you in good spirits?" I asked looking up into his eyes that sparkled like that of the surface of water that is struck by a ray of sunlight.

"There are many reasons for my joy, one being your mother for I long to see my beloved. Another being God's grace and mercy for he has shown favor upon us on our travels. I am also excited about finishing the house, getting back to work on it brings my heart joy." Father explained as he looked into the sky, I could see the side of his cheek extend past his face because his smile was so big.

"I miss mother too, how long do you think it will take to finish the house?" I asked eagerly.

"It will take about two months." Father swiftly answered.

I knew it would be a lot of work, but the thought of having our own home living inside of four walls made me that such more excited to finish it.

With both of them eager to get home, they traveled through the night only stopping briefly to feed Sampson and to relieve themselves. Before long, they could see the Sea of Galilee not too far off in the distance. Yeshai picked up the pace towards home as he began to recognize all the familiar terrain. They finally up the river from where they lived, the unfinished house laid next to their tent. Yeshai called out for his mother and began running towards their home. After a few minutes, Sabella emerged from the tent and when she noticed Yeshai and Jesus coming, she dropped everything she had in her hands and ran after them. Yeshai reached her first of course, embracing her extremely tightly.

"Mom, I've missed you!" Yeshai cried out as Sabella held him in her arms.

"I've missed you too, my little man of God, oh how I've missed you." She replied kissing him on the top of his head.

Shortly afterwards Jesus caught up to them and held both of them closely. The sun began to turn an amber orange color, which was reflected off of the surface of the water.

"My beloved, I have missed you so!" *Jesus told Sabella as he gently stroked her face with his fingertips.*

"My heart, And I you!" *Sabella began to cry.*

After they finished their heartfelt reunion, they all began walking towards the tent holding each other's hand.

"Mother I have so much to tell you!" I exclaimed with excitement.

"Really now, well I want to know all about you trip to Grandmother Mary's house. How is she by the way?" She gently replied as if she was concerned.

"OK! Nevertheless, I will have to tell you tomorrow because I am tired from long trip.

"That is fine, and I will tell you how my week has been also." She replied rubbing my head.

I looked around and saw everything just as we had left it. The water, the flowers, the gentle breeze passing across my face. I took a moment to take it all in, especially the sight of my parents together or working on the house. I saw mother smile and I saw father smile, and in that moment, I knew that I was home.

A house can only become a home with true love; the love of family but most of all the Love of God.
-Prophet

Chapter 10:

Reunion

*T*ime seemed to freeze as the family approached the unfinished home. The sun casted a golden overcast hills and plains. The birds seemed to be flying in one direction towards the warmth of the sun as if they were trying to catch it before it disappeared behind the mountains.

It felt good to be home, not 5 minutes after arriving I already had my wooden toy with me in hand. Mother led us to where she had prepared dinner, so we sat and ate together.

"So tell me about the adventure you two had?" She asked with a smile as she poured soup into our bowls.

"Where do I start?" I shouted with excitement.

She could tell how excited I was to fill her in on the details; she knows I love to talk to her about different things.

"Um let's see, you can start from your journey to Grandmother Mary's house. So how was that?" She said folding her arms and placing her index finger on her chin.

"Alright, well we were on our way and a man came out and had a sword!" I said eagerly attempting to build suspense.

"Oh really, he had a sword?" She asked quickly looking over to father and then back to me with a surprised look on her face to entertain my attempt at storytelling.

"Yea he tried to take our things but father talked to him. Then we helped him after father wrote forgiveness on the ground and the man cried!" I said speaking with my hands trying to draw a better picture.

"Who was this man?" she asked looking at the both of us.

"A man tried to take our belongings, but God had already informed me of the encounter so when he emerged from behind the broken wagon I knew his heart." Father explained, he looked like he wanted to say more to mother about it but instead he nodded his head and she did so in return.

"Yes and Sampson ate apples, and drank lots of water." I added.

"I'm sure Sampson was excited to get his favorite treat, what happened while at Grandmother's house?" She asked.

The food was delicious, I could hardly talk and eat at the same time, but I managed to make due.

"I saw Naomi and we played with the other children. We jumped in piles of hay and Naomi bout a bird!" I exclaimed.

"Oh my sweet Naomi how is she?" She asked.

"She is doing well." I answered.

"Her mother sends her regards and says she cannot wait until you come to visit again." Father added.

"Oh how I miss her, yes I must come with you two the next time you come to visit." Mother replied as she tore a piece of bread and handed it to father.

"Yeshai tell mother of the work you two did at the temple." Father suggested.

"You two?" Mother intuitively asked.

"Yes Naomi and I, she came along with us to help work on the temple roof. It was so fun, father taught us so much and she catches on quick. She should help us with our house." I answered pointing over to the unfinished project to the right of us.

"Sounds like you guys had quite an adventure. How is my mother?" She asked father.

"Mary is well, in good health and in good spirits." Father answered smiling as he dipped a piece of bread into the soup and ate it.

"Wonderful, well I'm sure you are tired from your journey, we should finish up here and get some rest." Said mother as she finished her soup.

"Yes ma'am, I am very tired." I answered letting out a yawn.

When we finished eating, we prayed and gave thanks. Afterwards mother set up my sleeping quarters and I played down in the back of the tent. Shortly afterwards both of them came inside and kissed me goodnight.

Within seconds Yeshai was fast asleep, Sabella and Jesus had finally laid down after putting away the supplies from dinner.

"So how are you husband?" *She sarcastically asked him.*

"I am well wife." *Jesus sarcastically responds.*
She pushes him in the arm and they both laugh.

"So what is this about a man trying to rob you two, what truly happened while you were away?" *She sternly asked removing all sense of sarcasm from her voice.*

"It's like I told you, Father came to me and informed me of what the man would do. Moreover, the enemy is contacting Yeshai. He has had dreams, visions, and has begun to ask questions about who he is. I can tell he is scared, who can expect anything less from a child his age." *Jesus explained placing his hand on Sabella's thigh.*

"Oh my, it seems it has begun. Yeshai is an intelligent and intuitive young one, he will continue to ask until he gets the answer he desires. What did you tell him?" *She asked placing her hand on top of his.*

"We did not answer his question fully; we thought it wasn't yet time. However, he is aware that he is not a normal child and that I am not a normal man. He spoke scripture to some teachers of the law back in Nazareth and they were amazed at his knowledge. The Holy Spirit is upon him and he has not yet fully understood the importance his life can have on others." *Jesus continued.*

"Already prophesying, I don't want him to miss out on a normal childhood; I want him to enjoy his youth." *She replied, as her demeanor appeared as if she began to worry.*

"I understand but he is no ordinary child, and his youth shall be as the Lord sees fit." *Jesus told her.*

"Does he know you are the Messiah?" *She asked placing her other hand on her head.*

"No, that has yet to be revealed to him. But he is close to knowing the full truth." *Jesus replied.*

"At least we have some time; no matter how little the amount of time that is at least we can see him enjoy his days before the responsibility of destiny is upon him. Oh I worry for him my love, I worry for you also." *She said full of concern.*

"Worry not my love, for he was made out of love. And love is what he shall spread." *He told her as he softly caressed the side of her face.*

Sabella held her head down slightly but Jesus lifted her chin and gently kissed her.

"You remove all worry with your touch and kiss. How could I restrain myself from your lips?" *She said as she kissed him back.*

Jesus gave her a look of assurance and held her in his arms. They continued to kiss and caress one another, as the night progressed they made passionate love. The flames of the lantern outside the tent, which was the only source of light besides the moon at this point, began to flicker and go out. In the morning, Sabella stayed asleep as Jesus and Yeshai began working on the house. The structure of the house was really starting to form.

"Father, can I ask you a question?" *Yeshai asked Jesus as he handed him a long sheet of wood.*

"Ask me anything." *Jesus assured him.*

Yeshai sat next to his father on the bench made from a sheet of wood held up by two piles of wood and other carpentry materials. Jesus could see the fire burning in his eyes, he had questions about what was happening to him and about who he was.

"Back when we were on our way to Grandmother's house, you said that God spoke to you and told you what would happen with that man. Did that have something to do with me?" *He sincerely asked looking up at his father.*

"Yes." *Jesus swiftly answered which reassured Yeshai that he was comfortable discussing these events.*

"How does God speak to you?" *Yeshai continued his barrage of questions.*

Jesus placed his hand on Yeshai's shoulder and held his other hand out in front of him.

"Sometimes I can hear his voice as clear as I can hear yours right now next to me. Other times I can understand through reading his word from the scriptures or he sends one of his angels to send me a message." *He explained looking into the palm of his hand.*

"What does the voice of God sound like?" *Yeshai questioned with fascination also looking into the palm of his father's hand.*

"It sounds like the crashing of thunder from a hundred storms and yet soft as a gentle gust of wind from a warm spring day. It is hard to put in words; you will understand when he speaks directly to you one day." *Jesus attempted to describe.*

"It's strange but that description seems familiar, like I've heard something similar to that before." *Yeshai replied with an intuitive look upon his face.*

They continued to sit and talk, Yeshai asked many questions regarding his father's past. Yeshai felt good knowing that his father trusted him with such information. He also enjoyed learning a little more about his life, after a while Sabella awoke and joined them.

"Good morning, what are my two favorite men up to over here?" *Sabella asked with a sweet smile.*

"Father and I are talking about everything that has been happening lately!" *Yeshai exclaimed in excitement.*

"Is that so, what is the current topic?" *She asked with slight suspicion.*

"Father was just telling me about the voice of God, it seemed familiar to me." *He told her as his eyes began to bulge.*

"Oh my, the voice of God!" *She exclaimed in an attempt to appease his excitement.*

"Yes, I feel like I heard it before!" *He energetically replied.*

Sabella and Jesus looked at each other, nodded in agreement first, and then turned to Yeshai.

"That is because you have." *They told him.*

"Really, the voice of God!?" *Yeshai asked in amazement.*

"Yes, when you were born God spoke to us." *They explained.*

"What did he say?" *Yeshai asked.*

Jesus allowed Sabella to speak on the subject.

"God told me that I would have a child, and that I was to name him Yeshai." *Sabella explained as she began to sit upright in reverence to the Lord.*

"I was named by God?" *He asked scratching his head.*

"Yes." *They answered him.*

"Does my name have meaning?" *Yeshai continued his questioning.*

"Yes, you name means the Word of God." *Jesus explained.*

"But I have never heard my name or its meaning before; not of the men in the scriptures or from anyone in our land." *Yeshai stated trying to make sense of the meaning.*

"This is because your name isn't like anyone in the scriptures nor is its meaning of any dialect in our land." *Jesus told him.*

"Did this meaning come from God?" *He asked carefully.*

"Yes, Yeshai comes from God, its origins lies in the heavens as his own language. In fact it is also the language of the angels, the Word of God in angelic tongue." *They told him.*

Yeshai was amazed at what he had heard, but the question began to rise in his heart as to why he was named by God.

"Why am I important enough to be named by God?" *Yeshai thought to himself.*

"I can see this is much for you to take in my love, perhaps we should have this discussion later." *Sabella suggested.*

"Yes, I have a lot to think about." *Yeshai agreed as he began picking up lumber and putting them in place.*

"Try not to worry about your name or everything that is happening around you too much, you are still a child and I want you to enjoy being a child." *Sabella told him as she began to clean up the area.*

Jesus resumed working on the house as well and they worked until midday. Sabella noticed a man walking up the road and went over to tell Jesus.

"My love, there is a man approaching from the main road." *She told him.*

Jesus stood up wiping his hands with a cloth rag as the man finally made it to them.

"Greeting traveler, how may we serve you?" *Jesus asked him.*

"Greeting, my name is Benjamin and I come from a small town to the south. There has been a plague in my land and so I lost my entire family to sickness. Now I travel begging from town to town for scraps to eat or money to buy food." *The man explained.*

Jesus was touched by the man, and asked him a question.

"Tell me; is your circumstance because you disobeyed God's law?" *He asked.*

"Um no sir, my circumstances are because of the plague. For I have followed God's law since a child and taught my family to follow in his ways." *Benjamin answered with his head partially bowed as a sign of respect.*

"Then why did the plague come and take away your family if not because of your sin?" *Jesus asked him.*

"That I cannot say kind sir, for the ways of the God are beyond my understanding. All I can say is that I'm sure that he has a plan and purpose for my circumstance." *He humbly replied.*

"What you say is true, your family was not lost because of your sin but because God has a plan and purpose for your life. Because you have remained humble even trough tribulation and have spoken truth, you shall never go hungry again, nor shall you travel from town to town to beg for anything." *Jesus assured him as he signaled for Sabella to bring him some food and water.*

"Thank you for such kind words." *Benjamin said earnestly.*

"Come we can give you food and drink, we do not have much but what we do have is yours, stay with us tonight." *Jesus eagerly told him.*

The man thanked him immensely and agreed to stay with them for the night.

<u>Regardless of your standing or situation, always do three things. Fear and Love the Lord your God. Love what your Lord God Loves. And finally read his word and spread the knowledge you have obtained to others so that they may know the Lord.</u>
-Prophet

Chapter 11:

Treasures of Heaven

*T*he evening came cautiously, the clouds that covered the sky slowly moved from east to west. The sun slowly set behind the horizon, and the moon gently took its place at the top of the sky. The waters were calm and the gently breeze caressed the land; flowing through the trees and blades of grass. After eating, Benjamin joined the Christs in the construction area.

"Thank you very much for the food and drink, I cannot remember the last time I've had the pleasure of tasting such an incredible meal!" *He complimented Sabella.*

"Oh thank you, you're quite welcome and please have as much as you like." *Sabella graciously offered.*

"So you all are building a house from the ground up, you must be a very talented carpenter because this work is amazing." *Benjamin told Jesus as he looked around at the walls and windows.*

"Thank you, we use the talents God gives us for his purpose. And maybe along the way of doing so we can enjoy the fruits of that labor as well." *Jesus responded as he handed Yeshai the hammer.*

"It looks like you the house is almost complete. How long have you been working on it?" *He asked.*

"About 6 months." *Jesus replied.*

"Yes father must be precise in every detail, every angle and measurement, every nail placed, every stone turned." *Yeshai explained.*

"I can tell that this home will definitely stand the test of time with such construction." *Benjamin added.*

"Yes it will for as long as it is intended to. Yeshai come down its getting dark, we can continue tomorrow." *Jesus said as he began picking up his tools.*

"Please allow me to help, it's the least I can do for your hospitality." *Benjamin told him as he picked up some as well.*

Very soon afterwards, everything was sorted and put in its proper place. Everyone was sitting around the fire enjoying the favorable weather; Benjamin had a look of peace upon his face as if he had not relaxed since the plague.

"Well Benjamin, tell us a little about yourself." *Sabella asked him as she snuggled underneath Jesus's arm.*

"Well I am from a very small village near Damascus. My family moved and settled in Ramla, Samaria when I was a small child. There I married and raised a family until about 6 months ago when the plague began." *Benjamin told them.*

"I am terribly sorry for your circumstance, what is your occupation?" *Sabella asked.*

I watched them speak to one another intensely as I sat with my wooden horse.

"I am a farmer, God allows my hands to work his land which brings forth crops from the soil." He told mother.

"Maybe you can teach me a thing or two about our garden." Mother chuckled making Mr. Benjamin laugh also.

"I would be honored to." He responded.

"You say that you are a farmer because you work the ground with your hands and God allows crops to grow from the soil. Do you know that God's people are also crops waiting to be planted and grown?" Father asked him.

"No, I have never thought of people in that way. How did you make that determination?" He responded with intrigue.

"God's people are lost, blinded by the sin of this world. So much so that even people who claim to be righteous just use his law for their own gain. Temple elders and teachers of the law take money for collections from the people yet there are those who are homeless and hungry. They wear illustrious robes and partake in large feasts in the name of the Lord but there are those who are sick and needy. Do they feed the hungry if not for their own gain, or help the homeless or the widow without a large crowd to lay witness to their deeds? No I say to you, even the "righteous" are tainted. Nevertheless, there are some who come in the name of the Lord who are like farmers that plants the seeds of his word into the hearts of God's people. Those who listen and accept truth are like ground the farmer works with his hands. And when they mature in the spirit they have the opportunity to plant more seeds themselves, just as a seed planted grows and produces a crop. So will God's people be produced from his word." Father explained in detail.

All of us stood in amazement at father's words, I looked over to mother, she seemed astonished herself, and she has heard father speak many times.

"How can such wisdom come from a man, good sir please tell me more? It seems that the Lord God has brought me to this place for a reason." He told him as he leaned in closer to the fire as to hear father better.

"All of these things and more can be revealed to God's chosen if we just open our hearts to listen to the voice of God." Father continued.

"Sir, you have welcomed me with open arms, allowed me to share food and drink with you and your wonderful family. You even have bestowed much wisdom onto my ears, please let me stay and serve you until the debt has been paid. I can help in the garden, tend to your colt, even assist with the construction of your home; just please allow me this act of repayment." Benjamin pleaded standing over the fire.

"Benjamin, how bright your light shines but is hidden behind a curtain like the sun behind the clouds. There is no debt to repay; all of these things have been given to you from God not I. The clothes you wear, the food you eat, and the water you drink are all provisions from the Lord. We must resemble God in kindness and in love, so there is no debt to repay. If you wish to stay for a time and help us around here I shall not get in the way of what God has placed on your heart to do, but let it not be out of debt but love." Father responded.

"Thank you sir and praise be to the God almighty for allowing our paths to cross in this way. However, I have to ask, earlier you told me that never again would I go hungry or travel from town to town begging. What did you mean by that?" He said as he walked over and sat by father's feet.

"Sometimes it is not meant for us to understand what the Lord's plans for our lives are but just to live them out and let his secrets be revealed in their appointed time." Father answered him.

In addition, just as I thought Benjamin might have asked another question, he looked up at father and nodded as if he understood what father meant. Afterwards mother and I helped set up another tent next to ours for Benjamin to sleep in and we all went to bed. The next morning I awoke to find father gone, he was over at the house working with Benjamin. I walked over to help but he told me that I had been working very hard and had the day to go and play. Mother came over as I began heading down to the river to play.

"Good morning Yeshai!" She called out to me as she waived.

"Good morning mother!" I shouted waving back.

"Good morning my love, and to you as well Benjamin. How did you sleep?" Sabella asked.

"Very well thank you ma'am, just thought I'd get an early start helping this morning only to find Jesus here already up and working." Benjamin joked.

"Well my husband enjoys early mornings; and knowing him, he has probably already meditated by now as well." *She teased.*

"You are correct my love I have already done so." *Jesus sarcastically replied.*

"I saw Yeshai walking down to the river, is he fetching water for breakfast?" *She asked.*

"No, I told him to take the day off and go and have fun. He has been working very hard and deserves to just enjoy himself." *He told her proudly.*

"Really, that was very considerate of you." *She complimented.*

"Well a wise woman once told me that it's important for the boy to have fun just being a child and having a normal childhood." *Jesus jokingly complimented her.*

"Well this woman must be very wise." *She joked in return.*

"Yes when she is not bickering too much." *He teased as he ran out from the house.*

"I do not bicker!" *Sabella snarled and chased after him.*

"Ha Ha true love." *Benjamin laughed as he picked up a stack of wood and placed them near the tools.*

Jesus continued making fun as he ran in underneath the ladder with Sabella in close pursuit. They ran around the entire house and then fell in the grass in laughter.

"Oh my, I will live a long and healthy life laughing with you." *She told him as she attempted to catch her breath in his arms.*

"Yes a long life indeed, Lord willing." *Jesus gasped for air holding her closely.*

I saw them running from the river, I could hear mother's threats, and she chased father. Father always knew how to get her started but always knew what to say to calm her down.

"Those two are always up to mischief, I can't wait to tell Grandma Mary the next time I see her." I thought to myself.

After playing for a while down at the river, I returned home for lunch. Benjamin and father had taken a break from working and came to eat as well.

"Let us eat." Mother shouted.

They ate and gave thanks to God and then returned to work. Over the next few weeks, Benjamin was a great help. He taught Sabella farming and irrigation techniques and assisted with the finishing touches on the home. Their garden grew and Jesus spoke many things about the Kingdom of God to Benjamin. He asked many questions and grew in wisdom and in the spirit.

"It is finished." *Jesus said as they stood in front of the completed house.*

It was of good size; it held five bedrooms and even had a 2nd floor. There was a nice view of the sea and surrounding area.

"It's beautiful!" *Sabella exclaimed.*

"Yes dad, I love it!" I added in excitement.

"I am sure you all are proud of such a magnificent structure. I have learned a lot these past few weeks past." *Benjamin said aloud.*

"So have we, thank you for all of your help." *Sabella said giving him a pat on his back.*

"It has been a blessing to have you with us, but now it is almost time we part ways." *Jesus told him.*

"Wait, he is leaving?" *Sabella asked with a look of confusion on her face.*

"Father, does Mr. Benjamin really have to go?" I asked with concern.

"It's quite alright little one, I understand. I truly appreciate all of the love and hospitality you have shown me. I can have my things ready to leave by morning." Benjamin assured mother and me.

"Benjamin isn't leaving rest assured." Father told us.

"But you said it's almost time to part ways?" We all asked him.

Then father smiled and pointed to the house and looked at all of us.

"Yes because we are the ones leaving, Benjamin will remain here." Father said with pleasure.

"I am confused, why would I stay here and you all leave? Where would you go? What is the meaning of this?" Benjamin babbled with bewilderment.

"Yes my love, what do you mean we will leave?" Mother added with a similar look as Mr. Benjamin.

"Family listen, the time has come for us to leave this place. All will be revealed in due time." Jesus explained.

"Ok my love I trust you, wherever you go I will go." Mother submitted.

"Mr. Benjamin must have been pretty lonely before going around by himself from town to town, it's just makes me sad that he will be left alone again." I said with my head down.

"It's ok child, for I won't be alone I will have the Lord as my company. But I still cannot believe you are leaving, you just completed your home!" Benjamin exclaimed.

"Benjamin won't be alone son, he will be with them." Father told me as he pointed off into the distance.

"Who's over there?" Mother asked shielding her face from the sun with her hand trying to look off into the distance.

"I cannot see from here." I added squinting my eyes.

"Keep looking." Father told us.

The figures became larger as they approached.

"Who are they?" Mother and I asked still trying to make out their identity.

"No it cannot be!" *Benjamin uttered.*

Benjamin burst into tears and ran after them in a full sprint screaming.

"It's my family! Dear God almighty, praise him it's my family!" *He shouted as he ran.*

The Lord teaches love because he is loving, he teaches kindness because he is kind. He teaches giving because he is generous, and he teaches mercy because he is merciful. Remember such things in this hateful, unkind, selfish, and merciless world.
-Prophet

Chapter 12:

Fellowship

*T*he tension and excitement in the air could be felt as Benjamin ran towards his family.

"Benjamin is that you!" *The woman shouted from across the way.*

"Yes it's me!" *Benjamin exclaimed in full stride.*

They began running to him also and all broke into tears upon contact. They embraced one another, his children crying his name, his wife clinching him tightly.

"That's his family?" I asked mother and father.

"Yes, it seems that way." Mother answered.

"What God has placed together let no man separate." Father said staring off at the reunion.

After a little while, they all walked back over to us.

"Jesus, Sabella; I would like for you to meet my family. This is my wife Ishmael, my daughter Sophia, and my two sons Paul and Ethan. Everyone this is Jesus, his wife Sabella, and their son Yeshai." Benjamin said as he sobbed his eyes still red from crying.

"It is very nice to meet all of you." Mother and Father replied.

"I thought you said your family was dead, that you lost them during the plague?" I ignorantly blurted out.

"Yeshai don't be inconsiderate." Mother snarled at me.

"It is ok, but that is the question that plagues my mind is well. How are you all here I was told that you had all perished?" Benjamin questioned turning to his family.

"We didn't have much and Sophia became very ill, I sent the boys out for food when the evacuation order came and everyone began to panic. Soon it was such crowds that people were being trampled on. We tried looking for you but could not find you. There was a family that died in the chaos and I assume whoever told you that we dies must have thought we were them. Afterwards we set out from place to place in hopes that we would run into you. Then I remembered that you being from Damascus might have returned there so here we are on our way there to find you. It has been so long, and we have traveled very far and to find you, I just thank the Lord that you are well." Sophia explained as tears began to flow once more.

"Yes it was John our neighbor who told me, he and his family were on their way out. He said that the bodies were so damaged that it was hard to identify them. When I tried to go look for myself and give you all a proper burial all the bodies that were found had already been stacked in the center of town and burned. The solders would even let me go home to get my things. So I wept and then wandered around lost begging until I found myself here with them." Benjamin explained holding them in his arms.

"No my love, we are alive and well. Thank you for taking care of my husband." Sophia told us.

"It was no trouble at all, he has been a huge help around here. Praise be to the God of our forefathers for reuniting you all." Sabella exclaimed.

"May we stay here tonight; we are tired from our long journey." Sophia asked kindly.

"Sophia, we may stay here as long as we like this is our home now." Benjamin told her.

"I do not understand, we could not possibly impose on them in such a way. We will rest and be on our way elsewhere." She told him.

"This is your home, it was built for you." Father told her.

"Built for us, I don't understand?" Sophia asked.

"This man is very wise and blessed by the Lord; he has taught me much during my time with them. He said that they are leaving and that this house is for us. Wait, how long ago did you say you started building this house?" Benjamin interrogated realizing the similarities between the two timeframes.

"About 8 months ago." *Jesus said with a smile.*

"That is such a coincidence, the plague happened about 8 months ago." *Benjamin explained trying to make sense of things.*

Mother looked over at father; he had the largest smile on his face. It was at that moment we knew what had happened.

"Sir, we do not understand." Paul and Ethan stated holding onto their parents.

"Father did you know they were going to come here all along?" I asked him.

"I was out in the field meditating and praying to the Father, and he told me of this day. He said go and build a house that would stand the test of time. For there will be some of my children who will live there, first you will be visited by a man. Soon after his family will come and they will serve me all of their days here. When you see the man know that your time has almost come. For you build this house and give it to them and as a result many will come to me." Father explained to us.

Jesus made it so Benjamin and his family could not hear what was said, for he did not want them to know who he was.

"Did you build this house for us?" Benjamin asked.

Therefore, Jesus gave this parable.

"There was a man who was living in extreme poverty and prayed every day to God not for himself but for the others living in that community. God was pleased by his selflessness and blessed him and he was given many riches. The man then went to where the poor gathered and gave those riches all away to them. This placed the man back into extreme poverty, and many for what he did mocked him. Some of the elders and teachers of the law asked why he did such a foolish thing, for he did not give but a portion of his wealth but all of it. He replied saying that all he has had belonged to God, and all he has now belongs to God. Why should he keep those richest only to himself? Is God not the God of all things? Will he not provide for me like he has all my life? Afterwards God took away their wealth and standing, and blessed the man even more so for his deeds; making him King over that land."

"The time has just come for us to leave here; I believe the Lord has plans for us elsewhere. You have helped build this house, you have worked the land around it, and you have become familiar with its surroundings. Who better to settle here in our stead than you and your family? Just remember the kindness we have shown you and do so for others. There are many out there in need, provide for them, there are many out there in the dark, shed your light upon them. There are many who do not know the ways of our father, tell them and show them just as I have shown you." *Jesus instructed him.*

"Yes, I will. But please do not leave today, at least stay the night with us. Let us feast and celebrate your hospitality and the reuniting of my family and praise the Lord for his glory." *Benjamin insisted as he began to clap his hands and dance praising God.*

"Very well we shall stay with you tonight and feast, we will leave tomorrow." Father agreed.

"Great, we can get to know each other, come inside." Mother said taking Sophia's hand into the house.

The men then moved all the belongings into the house, and the women began preparing dinner.

"Must we put everything in here; will you not take any provisions with you on your travels?" Benjamin asked father.

"We will one take the clothes on our back and some food and water with us tomorrow, everything else is yours including Sampson our colt. He will prove helpful as you tend to your crops." Father replied.

It saddened me that we would be leaving everything behind, but I began to understand why we were giving it all away. Therefore, I walked over to Ethan, Benjamin's youngest son, and gave him my toy wooden horse.

"Here you go, this was my favorite toy. My father made it for me, but I don't need it anymore." I told him nonchalantly as I handed it over.

"Thank you." Ethan replied.

Father looked at me and nodded in approval and we all went inside the house. While inside the boys played in the back room while the mothers began preparing the feast.

"I'm sorry I just can't stop crying, this entire day has been overwhelmed with all kinds of emotions. Just before we got here, I broke down into tears because I had almost given up hope that we would find Benjamin or even make it to Damascus. Then to even see him in the flesh standing in front of me, I could reach out and touch him was just such a blessing for our family. And to be given such a gift on top of all of this with meeting such blessed people like yourselves takes my breath away." *Sophia rambled in an emotional flurry.*

"We understand, it is a lot to take in all at once but praise God for reuniting your family and for blessing you with this beautiful home and surrounding land. For he is worthy to be praised, great are his mercies and his love shines down on those whom he shows favor. We are just as blessed as you to be able to be the instrument God used in his plan, and we are excited to know what the next chapter of our lives in him will be and take us." *Sabella sympathetically reassured her.*

"You are truly an angel from heaven, such kind, and loving words filled with such wisdom. Jesus must be truly honored for God to show favor on him and bless him with such a wife!" Sophia complimented placing her hand on Sabella's shoulder.

"Truly I am blessed; Sabella is such a miracle to have. She is a wonderful wife and mother to Yeshai and me." *Jesus politely interjected.*

"You two shower me with kind words, but it is I who is blessed to have Jesus." Sabella replied looking into Jesus eyes. For she knew what it meant to be chosen to be given in marriage to the Son of Man.

"Jesus I am overjoyed to be here with you all this evening. We shall feast together, fellowship in his Holy name and sings songs of praise so that even the angels in heaven will dance!" *Benjamin shouted.*

I looked around the house and smiled, everyone was joyful and enjoying the moment. Father was smiling and clapping his hands as everyone began to sing hymns to the Lord. There were no instruments at play but one would think the horns were sounding, the lyre was at work, and the trumpets were being blown in a beautiful symphony. I remembered this Psalm from one of fathers teaching as we all joined in song singing;

"Give thanks to the LORD, for he is good;
    his love endures forever.
Let Israel say:
    "His love endures forever."

Let the house of Aaron say:
 "His love endures forever."
Let those who fear the LORD say:
 "His love endures forever."
Blessed is he who comes in the name of the LORD.
From the house of the LORD, we bless you.
The LORD is God,
 and he has made his light shine on us.
With boughs in hand, join in the festal procession
 up[c] to the horns of the altar.
You are my God, and I will praise you;
 you are my God, and I will exalt you.
Give thanks to the LORD, for he is good;
 his love endures forever."

 The pleasant sounds onto the Lord bounced of every wall and we danced and sang for some time before it was finally time to sit and eat. We all sat at the head table father built, it was sturdy built of heavy wood able to sit ten people. With the food placed before us, we prayed and gave thanks to the Lord for his many blessings and provisions. Father prayed for the Benjamin family and mother gave thanks for everyone there. The food was delicious, it turns out Mrs. Sophia was an amazing cook as well. I knew her and mother would make good friends, even though we were leaving in the morning. And while thinking of leaving for a moment I became saddened not knowing what to expect. The fear of the unknown can be a terrifying thing.

"Father where will we go once we leave here?" I softly asked as to not ruin the mood of the party.

"Back to Nazareth to get you Grandmother." He sharply replied.

Mother looked at him and immediately knew why he said what he said. For I wanted to know what they were thinking but I dared not ask another question.

"Jesus, thank you again for everything you have done. Know that you always have a home here with us should you ever need it." Benjamin said proudly.

"Thank you Benjamin, for the Kingdom of heaven shall open its doors to those such as you." Father replied with a smile.

After dinner, the boys, and I helped, the adults clean up and put everything in its proper place. The hour was getting late and I could feel the fatigue of the day's events set in. My eyes became heavy and it looked as though I was not the only one. It was time for bed, time to go to sleep to regain my strength to get ready for what was ahead. For tomorrow will bring the unknown, a new chapter of my life, and I was excited to face it!

**One never fully realizes the Lord's hands at work on their behalf until everything comes full circle into fruition. So take the time to thank the Lord, thank him for the many blessings you see as well as those you do not see because his hands are always at work on your behalf.**
**-Prophet**

Chapter 13:

The Will of God

It felt as if the sun shot up into the sky in a flash of light, or maybe it was just my excitement knowing we were about to go to Nazareth of Galilee, as a family and experience whatever father had planned for us. It was crazy here we were spending months building this house and yet we were not even going to live in it. All the hard work sweating in the hot sun, every nail held a story just waiting to be shared with the world only to be given away. Surprisingly this did not bother me; it was as if God was working on my heart not to be attached to the house so that when it was time to part with it, it would not weigh heavy on me.

"Do we have everything ready my love?" Mother asked father as she walked into the room.

"Yes dear, we are not taking much with us. Fill that wine skin with water and take a few loaves of bread and some meat from last night's feast and we shall be on our way.

"What can I do to help?" I asked in an attempt to be useful.

"Wake the others up, for we will pray before we live and say goodbye." Father told me so I did as he told me.

I ran upstairs to one of the bedrooms to wake the boys and noticed that Benjamin was already awake getting ready to come down.

"Good morning Yeshai, I guess today is the big day for you all." He said in passing.

My face tried to remain neutral as I replied as calmly as I could.

"Yes I suppose it is." I replied trying to remain calm.

"Ha ha, I can see the excitement practically about to burst out of you, its ok Yeshai I am happy for you all."

A sense of relief flashed across my body, and I could relax.

"Thank you sir, I can't wait to leave!" I exclaimed as I began to bounce around.

"Sophia just woke up, she will be down shortly, and will you be having breakfast before you leave on your travels?" Benjamin asked.

"I'm not sure; I will have to ask father and mother." I answered.

Then I proceeded downstairs to see what else I could do to help.

"Mother will we be having breakfast before we leave?" I asked sincerely.

"No it is fine, father says what we will bring will suffice for breakfast for we are already provided for." She replied to my question.

After a few preparations, we were all ready to go. We stood out in front of the house to give our "goodbyes" or as mother would say our "see you laters." Everyone embraced one another and we prayed for a safe journey and traveling mercies.

"It has truly been a blessing meeting all of you." Sophia and Benjamin shouted as we began leaving.

"And to you all as well." We replied waving as we began to fade from view.

We began heading down the road holding each other's hand with me in between mother and father. I had seen the scenery many times but for some reason this trip felt different. Maybe it was because this time we were not going to visit and return home but heading out on an adventure instead.

"What seems to be the matter my little man of God?" Mother asked with a smile.

"I've just never left home for good before." I replied with my eyes downcast shortly before lighting up with excitement.

"Yes, it will take some getting used to but I can tell you are excited to see what happens next." Father told me swinging my arm back and forth, as we walked.

I then realized that I have lived my entire life in Galilee, but my roots where in Nazareth and I became interested.

"Father?" I casted out the like of my inquisition hoping that he would take interest and bite.

"Yes son." He answered receptively.

"Why did we not live in Nazareth with Grandmother, why live so far away?" I asked in hopes not to come off disrespectful.

"That is quite a question; I suppose it may have been easier to stay in the town close to her huh?" He said placing his hand on my head and smirking over to mother.

"Yes, it just makes more sense to me." I swiftly responded noticing there was some sort of humor to my question.

"Listen, I do not mean to offend you Yeshai, when a man marries he is to leave his father and mother and cling to his wife and they shall become one because what God puts together let no man separate." Father explained as he straightened the humorous expression on his face sensing my frustration.

"But what does that mean father?" I asked trying to understand.

"You see, before I married your mother I lived with my parents. They raised me and when I became of age my father became ill and passed away. After that, I stayed to help my mother with whatever she needed but there came a time when I had to move on with my life. I met your mother we later married; afterwards your Grandmother knew that I had to leave because my obligation was now to my wife. Understanding this herself, I offered for her to live with us but she refused and I respected her decision but I had to go and start a family. I stayed close enough just in case she needed me but far away to be independent in regards to fulfilling what was meant for me. Then we had you and jus settled in what we had made our home." He explained further.

"So you had to leave?" I asked beginning to grasp the concept.

"Yes, your father and I chose to leave. I also left my father and mother started my life with him. Once you marry your obligation is to God and each other." Mother politely interjected to help me understand.

"Yes exactly, thank you my love. I was born in Bethlehem, and shortly after that, my parents brought me to Egypt for a time before returning to this land and living in Nazareth. I guess seeing other places in my youth helped the decision to leave. I wanted to see more of the land outside of Nazareth." Father said with his words filled with gratitude.

"You're welcome darling, does that make sense Yeshai?" She asked me.

"Yes, I guess so." I replied giving the vibe that their answers where good enough for me.

With all of the questions and conversation, it had not occurred to me just how much ground we had covered. We had made it over halfway there before the sun began to set.

"May we stop and rest for the night, we traveled very far, and Yeshai is exhausted." Mother mentioned to father.

"Of course, the hour is getting late; we will make camp just over the next ridge. There is a spot that we can make camp and rest until morning." He obliged her.

They made it over the ridge and set up camp to rest. Yeshai immediately fell asleep. The next day they headed back out early and made it to Nazareth. Once they arrived at Mary's house they were greeted with overwhelming hospitality.

"Praise God! As I live and breathe is that you Sabella!?" Mary exclaimed trying to get a good look at her.

"Yes mother it is I, how good it is to see you!" She returned the enthusiasm.

They embraced one another and both broke into tears.

"It is very good to see you son! And you as well my little Yeshai!" She shouted with joy.

"It is good to see you as well Grandmother." I replied trying to breathe through her tight embrace.

"How have you been mother?" Father asked her as he embraced her.

"I have been well; God has provided me with all that I require." She answered.

"Good, good, it brings my heart joy to see you basking in his favor." Father said as he closed the door behind us.

"So what brings you back so soon, and all of you? I thought you were not going to return until after you finished the house?" She asked.

"The house is already finished Grandmother." I said proudly.

"Oh my! You two must have been breaking your backs to finish so far ahead of schedule." She complimented us with concern.

"We had some help from a man by the name of Benjamin." Father told her.

"Oh I see, but why doesn't this feel like your normal visit to me?" She inquired as she sat down at the table.

"This is because it isn't mother." Father said bringing us all together underneath his arms facing mother.

"So what is the purpose of this visit?" She asked looking at all of us huddled together.

"Mother, it is time." Father said powerfully.

I looked at Grandmother and she paused for a moment, and then acknowledged father's words without question and immediately began gathering her things.

"What is she doing?" I thought to myself.

"When do we leave?" Grandmother asked him.

"In the morning." He replied.

"Very well." Grandmother said as she continued gathering her things.

"Why is she doing that father, are we not staying here?" I asked.

"No, we are all leaving together tomorrow." He answered me in such a way I dared not ask another question about the subject not from fear but respect.

I always knew my father would share with me what was going on when he was ready to do so.

"Yes sir, may I go play with Naomi?" I asked.

"Of course son." Mother quickly answered me opening the door.

And with the swiftness of a rabbit I was out the door and down the street. I ran to Naomi's door and knocked out of breath. Her father answered and greeted me.

"Yeshai, it is very nice to see you. Naomi come to the door." He called to Naomi.

Naomi came to the door and was shocked to see me.

"Hi Naomi." I murmured, still out of breath.

"Hello Yeshai, how have you been?" She asked as if she just saw me yesterday.

"I am well; my family is here to get my Grandmother." I explained.

"Oh, where are you taking her?" She asked.

"I am not sure where we are going from here." I answered.

"Oh my, you are taking Mary from us?" Susanna asked emerging from the back of the house.

Realizing that I probably said too much, I attempted to change the subject.

"Um, can Naomi come out to play?" I said crossing my fingers.

"Sure, you too have fun. Yeshai is your mother here?" Naomi's mother asked me.

"Yes ma'am she is." I answered still trying to get away.

"Please tell her I said hello, and tell your father that he owes us dinner." She shouted as we ran away.

"Looks like we are all eating together tonight ha ha." Naomi said as we ran.

"Ha ha yup, your mother isn't one I would want to see angry, she scares me." I laughed.

We ran up near the open fields and sat underneath a tree.

"So you guys are leaving, do you know when you will return?" Naomi asked picking up a rock and tossing it over into the brush.

"I really don't know, this all just happened the other day. One minute we are finishing the house and the next we are leaving everything behind to come here to get Grandmother." I tried to explain.

"Wow that is crazy, speaking of leaving everything behind where is your toy horse?" She asked.

"I gave it away." I replied.

"You mean to tell me that you were able to part with that thing?" She replied astonished.

"Sure tease away, your insults will not bother me this time. The little boy looked like he needed it more than me." I sternly responded.

"Look at you Yeshai, you are growing up." She complimented.

"Really you think so?" I asked feeling good from her compliment.

"Yea you went from being a child with a slightly enlarged head who likes toys to just a child with a slightly enlarged head. You are maturing ha ha!" She strategically teased him.

"Oh why did I even go to your house if all you are going to do is make fun!?" I snapped feeling embarrassed realizing that she drew me in and set me up for the insult even while I was on guard.

Expecting a cold response to my reaction Naomi actually surprised me by embracing me.

"I am sorry Yeshai, I went too far with my joke." Naomi said sincerely.

"It is ok." I replied.

"It isn't fun not knowing when I will see my best friend again." She said looking away from me.

This was not like her; she never turned away from me before to I grabbed her arm and turned her back towards me to find that her eyes were watery. Tears began falling down like raindrops in a soft squall.

"Don't cry, I'm sure we will see each other again soon." I attempted to console her.

"Yea I know, I can't believe I am crying." She quickly wiped her eyes and stood up.

We then headed back and stopped at Grandmother's house to relay the message from Susanna.

"Mother Susanna wants to see you, and she says that father owes them dinner." I told them

"Do you think we have time for dinner tonight?" Mother asked father.

"I don't see why not." He replied.

"Hello Naomi, my how you have grown. It has been too long." Mother told her as she gave her a hug.

Father also greeted her with a hug and then went back into the house to help Grandmother gather her things.

"It was great to see you Naomi, tell your parents that we would love to have dinner with them here." Mother told her as we began to leave.

We wandered off to play a little longer near Naomi's house and then it was time to prepare for dinner so I headed back. Walking through the door I was met with the sweetest aroma from what was being prepared. Instantly my stomach began to rumble.

"Oh my goodness, Grandmother and mother must be trying to attract the angels to dinner with this smell." I thought to myself.

"Come and freshen up for dinner Yeshai." Mother called to me.

"Yes ma'am." I said heading to the back towards her.

Shortly afterwards dinner was nearly ready when they heard a knock at the door. Jesus answered the door and it was Naomi and her family carrying a loaf of bread and some wine.

"Welcome, it is very good to see you all. Come inside and have a seat." Jesus greeted them with open arms.

"Thank you." They all replied as they entered the house and sat down.

"Everyone here together, sharing stories and having dinner. Oh this is going to be a great night!" Yeshai thought to himself.

As Jesus shut the door behind them, the sweet smell of the bread carried out into the street as the sun began its decent into the mountain pass.

Sometimes closing a chapter in the book of life prepares us to open another chapter with each new page filled with fun and amazing experiences to create a story.
-Prophet

Chapter 14:

John the Baptist

*A*s the blanket of light from the sun began to unfold itself behind the horizon, there was a hint of joy in the air. A since of quiet peace that floated throughout the land like a gently kiss as the lips come into contact with the skin.

"How good it is to see you all again." *Susanna told them as everyone began sitting at the table to eat.*

"Yes what a fine day it is to have such good company with loved ones." *Sabella replied as she clapped her hands together with gratitude.*

"Thank you for preparing this mean Grandmother and mother." I thanked them.

"Oh you are very welcome." They responded identically and laughed realizing what just happened.

"Are you sure you didn't give birth to Sabella as well mother?" Father teased.

"Oh be silent, don't say such things Jesus." Grandmother humorously scowled at him and waiving her hand to gently slap his arm.

Everyone began to laugh as we shared stories and continued the various conversations.

"So Mary have you heard?" Susanna casted the line of juicy discussion out in hopes that she would bite.

"Heard of what?" Mary replied.

"A man named John is out in the wilderness near the Jordan river preaching to large crowds and proclaiming the coming of the Messiah!" She told her with enthusiasm.

"Oh I thought I heard something similar to that just the other day, but they said there was a wild man in the wilderness blaspheming against the scriptures. They did not mention his name was John." Mary responded.

"Yes his name is John, John the Baptist." She added.

"Mother, isn't he my relative?" Father asked.

"Yes son, you two were born a few months apart. I actually stayed with his mother for some time while I was pregnant with you." Grandmother explained.

"I remember we used to play together as children, similar to you and Naomi son." Father told me with a smile.

"Why haven't I met him father?" I asked.

"I'm not sure, once we settled in Nazareth he and his mother moved to another town in Galilee so we didn't see each other much." Father explained.

"I don't know whether to call this John the Baptist a prophet or a mad man." Aaron jokingly stated.

"I can assure you, he is no mad man, tell me more about what he is doing?" Father asked Susanna.

"All I know is what I've heard, they say that he is baptizing people in the river and is gaining the attention of the elder's the temple." She responded giving visual aids with her hands.

"We must go there at once; truly this man is whom I must see." Father said placing his hand on Sabella's shoulder.

"Why would you want to go see him?" Aaron asked with a confusing look on his face.

"We are leaving this place in the morning, and the message that John has must be delivered to me." Father told him.

Aaron laughed and was about to mock Jesus for not making any sense but just as he touched his arm, a flood of truth came into him. He was made aware of whom Jesus was and a look of awe came across his face.

"Is everything ok darling?" Susanna asked him.

"Um, uh, I don't know." Aaron tried to clear his throat and began to sweat.

"Daddy you are acting strange." Naomi told him.

"Yes dear are you sure that everything is ok?" Susanna asked with increasing concern.

Aaron looked over at my father and slowly nodded. Mother and Grandmother both paused and then became silent; I could not understand why everyone was acting strange. Naomi looked over to me in complete bewilderment, as father turned to Susanna with a smile.

"Susanna everything is alright, Aaron has just come into the truth." Father told her.

"What truth?" She asked.

"Why he must go to see John." Aaron politely interjected.

"I am not sure of what you two mean, but we can discuss it later after we eat if you wish." She replied.

"Yes, let us eat." Grandmother strongly suggested.

She signaled to Mother to bring the food over to the table and we all gave thanks. As we began to eat, both Naomi and I were bursting inside to know what the big secret in the room was.

"When do you all plan to return?" Susanna asked before taking a bite of food.

"I am not sure." Mother told her dipping the bread into the broth.

"It was very nice to see all of you at once; we should do this more often when time permits." Susanna continued.

Everyone agreed as they continued eating.

"Father, so we will go to see this John?" I asked in an attempt to unravel the mystery of the secret at the table.

"Yes, we will leave tomorrow and then more will be revealed to you." Father answered me in a way that allowed no further questions.

Naomi looked over to me with a frown insinuating that I had given up too easily, but I returned her look with a look of my own. This look insinuated that she does not know who we are dealing with. She finally left me be and continued eating her meal. After dinner, father and I cleared the table and we all walked Naomi and her family to the door.

"Praise God for such a blessed evening." Grandmother stated as she gave Naomi and Susanna a hug.

"Yes all praise be to him who has given us life and brought us together this evening." Aaron replied as he gave her a hug in return.

"When you all return come and find me so we can play ok?" Naomi said as she hugged me and slipped a piece of paper into my pocket.

"Of course, just try and keep up this time he he." I teased in a corny attempt to hide the fact that she passed me a note.

Everyone said his or her goodbyes and Naomi and her family went home.

"I will help clean up." I said with my face downcast.

"Thank you my little man of God." Mother replied in an attempt to cheer me up.

"Yeshai, it is alright, you will see Naomi again." Grandmother casted a line of encouragement in my direction.

I knew they were just trying to take my mind off the situation and I really was excited about leaving but in that moment realizing that I did not know the next time I would see her really troubled me. After cleaning up, I went to lie down and stared at the ceiling. A lot has happened in this past year, it felt like yesterday that we were living peacefully along the side of the river. Now so much has happened that I cannot explain, and the feelings that have been lingering in my heart have had me questioning everything I ever knew. I still did not know who the man in the dark hood was, and I still did not understand what he meant when he said "Ask him who he is."

"Yeshai worry not, you will see Naomi again soon." Father told me as he lay down and closed his eyes.

Yeshai was exhausted emotionally and not understanding how to cope with the current situation, he just drifted off to sleep. The next morning everything was packed and ready to go for the trip. Mary also did not take much instead entrusted her house and belongings to a neighbor of hers in her absence. As the exited the house to begin their travels they were met by Naomi and her family. They stood there in the road waiting for them with bags of their own as if they were about to travel.

"Naomi?" I thought to myself seeing her standing there next to her mother and father.

"Susanna, where are you all headed so early?" Sabella asked her.

"Oh why with you of course." She replied with a smile.

"With us?" Mother replied with a stunned look on her face.

"If you would permit us to do so?" Aaron asked Jesus.

"Why refuse you, it would bring my heart joy to see you all travel with us." Father answered warmly.

"This is great!" I exclaimed with the largest smile I could muster.

"Ha ha Yeshai and Naomi seem to be in good spirits." Father joked.

"But what made you decide to come with us?" Mother asked Aaron.

"Last night after leaving I thought a lot what your husband said and discussed it with Susanna. She thought I was a mad man by the idea of picking everything up to come with you but I explained to her the situation and she agreed. So at first light I got up and went to the man who offered to buy my house and all my land a few weeks back and offered it all to him. He accepted and so here we are with a few bags ready and willing to serve." Aaron explained.

"You sold everything to follow Jesus? What did you do with the money?" Mother asked in awe.

"Yes, yes we did and we gave it all to the poor. We were blessed to have some silver to purchase a few things for the journey but overall yes we did." Aaron respectfully answered.

"I don't understand why but at least I get to play with you Yeshai." *Naomi said shrugging her shoulders.*

"I couldn't make sense of what he was sharing with me about last night, but he believes in Jesus and I believe in him." *Susanna explained.*

"Wow, I am at a loss for words, praise be to the almighty God who places our feet on solid ground and gives us such beloved friends to share this journey with!" *Sabella shouted in praise.*

"Truly I tell you, many will knock at the door of the Kingdom of heaven but few will be allowed to enter into its gates. This day you have pleased the Father and he will allow a place to be prepared for you in the Kingdom." *Jesus told them with open arms.*

"My God, every day you surprise me and every day I see your many blessings and everlasting favor." *Mary joined in praise.*

"Let's go, let's go!" I exclaimed in excitement as I began skipping down the road with Naomi.

"Ha ha alright let us leave; we will see what the will of God has in store for us. You see Yeshai, I told you that you would see Naomi again soon," Father said winking at me as he placed his arm around mother's shoulders.

And they all began walking in the direction of Judea near the place that the rumors of John the Baptist was describing. As they traveled from place to place, Naomi and Yeshai played to their hearts content. Sabella and Susanna conversed with Mary and each other talking about many different topics. And Aaron stayed very close to Jesus asking him various questions about salvation.

"Jesus, Lord, can I ask you a question?" *Aaron whispered so that the children would not hear him.*

"Yes, what is it?" *Jesus answered turning to face him as they walked.*

"When I touched your arm last night all of a sudden everything came flooding into my mind and heart. It is like in that moment everything became clear to me. I felt like God was telling me to follow you. What happened last night?" *Aaron asked sincerely.*

"Aaron, you are an upright man who follows God's commands but you are so skeptical. God chose to reveal who I am to you so that you may bear witness to the great works. You will see firsthand why he is God and be rid of all of the doubt in your heart. He has chosen you and your family for his purpose to follow me and testify to others the truth about the Kingdom of God." *Jesus explained to him.*

"Thank you Lord, I understand." *Aaron respectfully submitted and continued walking.*

They traveled very far and set up camp during each night. Each morning after eating, they continued their journey along the road. They crossed the rivers and streams of Galilee, which lead into the open plains near Nain. They traveled over the hills and around the base of the mountains that bored the land of Samaria. Jesus would often speak to the group about the Kingdom of heaven and the two families became even closer. While in Samaria, they camped along the mountainside inside a cavern for the night that overlooked the Sycharian valley near Mt. Gerizzin.

"We will travel along the Jordon until we come to the valley where people are coming to hear him speak and be baptized." *Jesus told them.*

Therefore, they did, they traveled for three days along the river until they finally came upon an open valley separated by the Jordan in Bethany. There were many people there listening to this man standing on the ridge speak. Everyone from the elderly to the small children was present and a smile came across Jesus's face.

"Father is this the place where we are supposed to come?" I asked looking up at him.

"Yes Yeshai, this is the place. Everyone gather around and listen to him speak." Father told us.

And we all sat near this large rock that wasn't too far from where he was preaching. He wore clothing made of camel's hair, with a leather belt and ate locusts and wild honey. There was a small group of men talking loudly while John began to speak and Jesus told them to be silent.

"After me come one even more powerful than I, one whose sandals straps I am unworthy to tie. I baptize you with water, but he will baptize you with the Holy Spirit." John shouted to the large crowd of people.

"Father, do we go to him?" I asked carefully.

"No, not yet, we must pay witness to what he is about to do." Father answered me.

John began speaking to the crowd saying.

"You brood of vipers! Who warned you to flee the coming wrath? Produce fruit in keeping with repentance. And do not begin to say to yourselves, "We have Abraham as our father." For I tell you that out of these stones God can raise up children for Abraham. The ax is already at the root of the trees, and every tree that does not produce good fruit will be cut down and thrown into the fire."

"What should we do then?" The crowd asked in a roar.

"Anyone who has two shirts should share with the one who has none, and anyone who has food should do the same." He replied.

Even tax collectors came to be baptized by him; standing in the crowd as well they asked him questions.

"Teacher, what should we do?" They asked.

"Do not collect any more than you are required to." He told them firmly.

There were some soldiers also in the crowd.

"And what should we do?" The soldiers asked earnestly.

"Don't extort money and do not accuse people falsely but rather be content with your pay." He instructed.

With such wise words, spoken Jesus was pleased; the people in the crowd began thinking in their hearts if John was possibly the Messiah but he told them that he was not and went on talking about the one to come after him.

"Surely this man is a prophet." A man called out from the crowd.

As he was speaking he looked outward into the crowd and saw us standing there listening to him. When he saw father he lifted his hands and his face instantly filled with excitement. He looked like he saw something miraculous and began to shout to the crowd to testify.

"A dove!? This is the one I spoke about when I said, 'He who comes after me has surpassed me because he was before me.' Out of his fullness, we have all received grace in place of grace already given. For the law was given through Moses, grace and truth came through Jesus Christ. No one has ever seen God, but the one and only Son, who is himself God and is in closest relationship with the Father, have made himself known!" John shouted with great joy.

The crown went into a state of amazement as many smaller squabbles began to take shape about someone actually being God.

"Who is this Christ?" A man shouted from the crowd.

"Yes who is he, where is he from?" Another man called out.

I began to get scared because some of the men looked angry and continued shouting.

John then began walking over in our direction when some priests sent by the Jewish leaders and Levites and questioned cut him off. He tried to continue past them but they were persistent and he ended up losing us from his sight.

"Who are you, are you the Messiah?" The men asked as they approached him.

"No, I am not the Messiah." John honestly responded.

"Then who are you, are you Elijah?" They continued questioning him.

"I am not." He responded firmly.

"Are you the Prophet?" They asked again.

"No." He said scanning the area behind them for Jesus.

"Then who are you? Tell us so that we can go back to the ones that sent us with an answer. What do you say about yourself?" They asked as their voices became to get filled with desperation.

"I am the voice of the one calling in the wilderness; make straight the way for the Lord." He responded quoting Isiah the prophet.

"Why then do you baptize if you are not the Messiah, nor Elijah, nor the Prophet?" They interrogated him.

"I baptize with water, but among you stand one you do not know. He is the one who comes after me, the straps of whose sandals I am not worthy to untie." He told them sternly.

We heard all of this from a distance and witnessed the priests become overwhelmed with frustration and stormed off to return to their homes. I was amazed at how sure he was about what he believed and his words came with such power.

"Why was he referring to by saying that my father as God?" I thought to myself.

Seeing the questions begin to pile up in my head through the expression on my face, father crouched down in front of me and placed his hand on my head.

"Yeshai, do not worry, for tomorrow everything about me shall be revealed to you." Father told me with a smile.

"Are we leaving here now?" I asked him.

"Yes only to rest for the night, we will return tomorrow and you shall see the glory of God." He replied as we began to exit through the crowd of people.

As we walked, those questions burned in my mind but I was excited because they would be answered tomorrow. I would learn of whom my father actually is, my father Jesus of Nazareth.

__Good are those that follow God's way, but great are those whom God's way flows from like a river through their words, actions, and testimonies.__
-Prophet

Chapter 15:

Truth

The sun's amber ambiance trickled off of the surface of the water like small pieces of broken glass. The clouds seemed to have departed, as the sky was now calm as the cool evening breeze was washing the intensity of the hot day. We walked further down the Jordan and spent the night facing the river. We were all tired from the long journey and were relieved to know we could finally get some rest. The furthest I had traveled was to Grandmother Mary's house and back and this trip was much longer than that. We prepared camp with some loose rags that Grandmother had packed for us and we lay in between two large rocks off the shore. As I lay there, I looked across the river and saw the dark hooded figure facing my direction. It looked as if it was signaling me to come over, but surprisingly this time no fear entered my heart. I stared back at the figure as if I was staring at myself in the mirror and drifted off to sleep.

"It appears that we were not the only ones to make the trip." *Jesus said to himself looking across the river and seeing the figure fade away into the darkness.*

The next morning we awoke and were surprised to see so many people up the river waiting for John to baptize and speak to them. So we headed back to where he spoke the day before, but they time he was there waiting for us to return.

"Jesus! My Lord!" He called out to father as we approached.

"John, cousin it is very good to see you." Father said with a pleasant smile on his face.

"I knew that you were coming but I did not know that the one I was waiting for would be my relative!" He exclaimed.

"The one you were waiting for?" Father asked him.

"Yes, the one who sent me to baptize with water told me, 'The man on whom you see the Spirit come down on and remain is the one who will baptize with the Holy Spirit.' And so as I spoke yesterday I saw this light shine around you and then I knew what had been foretold was at hand!" John explained as his eyes began to enlarge with every word.

"I knew that I would meet the one who comes before me to make the way, but I was not aware that it was my relative either. So it brings my heart even more joy to know that you cousin are that one." Father told him.

I stood listening in complete awe because I had yet to understand what was in fact happening around me.

"We have much to discuss between us." John told father.

"Yes we do." He replied.

"How long has it been since last we saw each other? Ten years? Fifteen?" He asked as we finally made it to him.

"Even more so, we were very young last we met." Father replied as he embraced him tightly.

"Aunt Mary, by the blessings of God looks at you, why you aged a bit." John complimented as he hugged her and kissed her on the cheek.

"Oh you are too kind, thank you; you have grown into a fine man." She told him, returning the hug and kiss.

"And who are these travelers with you?" He asked scanning his eyes across our group and landing them on me.

"This is my family, John Sabella my wife and Yeshai my son. This young lady is Naomi, Yeshai's best friend and her parents Aaron and Susanna. They have decided to sell all they have and follow me." Father explained as he introduced us as we all exchanged hugs with him.

"Well praise God! The time has come for you to proclaim the good news and begin your coming Kingdom." He told father as he ruffled my hair with his hand.

"Yes, but first there is something we must do." Father said stood out in front of us and stood next to john.

"What it is Lord?" John asked.

"You shall baptize me." Father instructed.

"But Lord, you are greater than I, shouldn't you baptize me?" John asked in respectful deterrence.

"You who say that I am greater than you should baptize you instead?" Father asked him.

"Yes, surely no one is qualified to baptize the Messiah." John suggested.

At that moment I began to grasp what was, they were talking about.

"Father, is he saying that you are the Messiah, the son of God?" I asked as my voice squeaked from the stress and tension of the sheer magnitude of the question.

"Yes he is son, remember when I told you that all will be revealed to you in due time?" Father asked me.

"Yes father." I replied bracing myself.

"What he says is true, I am the Messiah." Father told me with full confidence and assurance.

I looked up at him, and instantly felt so small and insignificant. His stature seemed to elevate above all of us in my eyes and soar high above the clouds themselves.

"My father? The Messiah? The Son of God! The same man that raised me, taught me carpentry and laughed with me until we both were in tears!? How could this be!?" I thought to myself, as I stood there frozen in bewilderment.

After the moment passed, I quickly turned and looked at mother and Grandmother for some sort of confirmation. Surely, they would have known this information too. As my eyes reached them, they just silently nodded in acknowledgement that what was said was true. Afterwards Aaron and Susanna also nodded, and Naomi stood there almost as stunned as I was.

"But you are my father, right?" I asked sluggishly, and as the words left my lips, I immediately regretted even asking the question.

"Ha ha yes Yeshai, I am still your father." He said as he laughed.

My entire life had been stripped apart and rebuilt in an instant, so many questions answered at once, and yet so many questions developed as a result of the answered questions. Every time I heard him mention God as the Father before all began to make sense now. He was not just speaking from a perspective of a believer regarding God as his Father because he is his creator. He was speaking from the perspective of a Son referring to his biological father.

"I know there are many questions yet to be answered, I ask that you give me time to answer them." Father kneeled down and faced me.

"Uh, yea of course father." I said astonished that he asked me earnestly with no insinuation of authority over me.

"Good, because first John must baptize me." Father told me as he stood to his feet.

"I need to be baptized by you, and do you come to me?" John told him.

"Let it be so now, it is proper for us to do this to fulfill all righteousness." Father explained looking at John.

"Very well Lord, I am your humble servant." John consented.

So right, there in the midst of everyone, including the people gathered to be baptized and spoken to by John; father and John walked into the water. We all walked to the water's edge, I could feel the cool water in between my toes, and rushing over my feet as the waves submerged them all the way up to my ankles. We all watched silently as John held my father in his arms floating on the surface of the water. John then pushed Jesus under and in that moment, it felt like father had been submerged for an eternity.

"My God!" Sabella blurted out as she watched Jesus remain underwater.

Then suddenly Jesus emerged from the water and a flash of unexplainable white light consumed the entire river. It was almost blinding, as if the sun had focused all its light on that one area. The wind began to blow harshly and the clouds above their heads in the sky began to part. The area in between the clouds contained this aura; it appeared to be heaven like. Then the wind stopped and out of that aura in the sky, a small white dove flew down and placed itself on the shoulder of Jesus. Finally, a loud voice rumbled from the heavens, and was so powerful that the ground beneath their feet shook and some lost their footing and fell.

"This is my Son, whom I love; with him I am well pleased." *The voice graciously rumbled through the land.*

All who heard this voice was astonished, fell to the ground, and worshipped God.

"My God, the Hold ruler!" Mary exclaimed at the sound of his voice.

I looked over at Naomi and she was terrified, as her parents were on their knees in worship. My body would not respond to my mind's commands, as I tried to move but could not. After the voice ended and the aura in the sky left as the clouds returned to their proper place father looked at me from the water. He did not say a word but his expression said it all. I knew then that he had a mission that was bigger than everyone of us was. Afterwards they walked back to the shore and the entire crown silent at what they had just witnessed began to crowd around waiting for another sign from God.

"These people, they see signs as entertainment and seek more for themselves instead of yet heading warning to the prophets teachings and fearing the Lord their God." John said aloud so the people could hear him.

Then two men who were close by walked over to us and stood next to John.

"Look, the Lamb of God." John told them.

Father embraced John and signaled us to start heading through the crown and back up the river. Once we cleared the crown John came and sat with us and ate with us and shared stories of him and father when they were children.

"Those were good times; it seems that now our paths are meant to part." John told father.

"Yes, but there is still so much work left for you to do." Father told him.

"I will continue to spread your message and baptize until my life has served its purpose." John replied proudly.

"Take very good care of yourself cousin, I love you." Father told him and he embraced him.

"And I love you as well my Lord." John replied with tears in his eyes, knowing that in his heart this would be the last time he saw Jesus alive.

After we ate, we began heading back down the river when we noticed the two men who was with John following us.

"What do you want?" Father asked them.

"Rabbi, where are you staying?" They asked.

"Come and you will see." He told them and we continued walking.

We came to the place where slept the night before and they stayed with us.

"What is your name?" I asked them.

"My name is Andrew, and this is John." He replied on their behalf.

"You have the same name as my relative." I told him.

"Yes that is true." John giggled.

And the two of them stayed with us until about four in the afternoon listening to Jesus speak to them.

"I must leave but I shall return shortly." Andrew said as he stood up and ran off into the distance.

John remained with us astonished by my father's words listened intently and asked many questions regarding salvation. Not too long afterwards, Andrew returned with another and sat with us.

"Simon, this is Jesus, the Messiah, whom I told you about." Andrew explained as he made the introduction.

"You are Simon, son of John, but you will be called Peter." Jesus told him.

Afterwards we all retired for the day. When we awoke father was ready to leave, he led us to a man named Philip.

"Follow me." He told him, and Phillip did so.

Later Philip found a man named Nathanael and told him:

"We have found the one Moses wrote about in the Law, and about whom the prophets also wrote. Jesus of Nazareth and the son of Joseph.

"Can anything good come from there?" Nathanael asked.

When Phillip brought him over and father saw him, he smiled.

"Here truly is an Israelite in whom there is no deceit." Father said openly to all of us.

"How do you know me?" Nathanael asked confused.

"I saw you while you were still under the fig tree before Phillip called you." Father told him with certainty.

"Rabbi, you are the Son of God and the King of Israel." Nathanael exclaimed as he fell to his knees.

"Rise my child, you believe because I told you that I saw you under the fig tree. You will see greater things than that. Very truly I tell you, you will see heaven open, and the angels of God ascending and descending on the Son of Man." He preached.

Phillip and Nathanael joined us as well headed towards Galilee, but on the way, we were stopped by a messenger.

"Excuse me; I have a message for you." The messenger said as he handed the paper to Jesus.

Father handed it to Grandmother and she read it.

"This is an invitation to a wedding in Cana; someone is getting married in two months' time." She said.

"Very well, thank you for the message young man, tell the one who sent you that we will attend this wedding." Father told the messenger as we continued walking.

Afterwards we found ourselves heading back towards Nazareth, but when it became dark father gathered everyone around the fire.

"Listen everyone, the work of the father is at hand and we will head to Nazareth to do his work but first I must do something alone." He told us as the flames of the fire danced to the sound of the winds gently purr.

"What must you do alone my love?" Mother asked with concern.

"I must go into the wilderness to pray and fast, when I return we will leave." He answered her.

"Do you know how long?" She asked.

"As long as it takes, the Father has a plan for me and until that plan is realized I must stay out there." He explained.

"When are you leaving?" I asked him.

"Tomorrow morning, while I am away I need you to take care of your mother and Grandmother. John I trust that you will keep everyone safe." Jesus told us.

We nodded and then father took me off by ourselves to talk.

"Now that you know who I am, how do you feel?" He asked me.

"Uh, um, it feels like this feeling I've had for so long in my stomach has just went away. I could never explain it, but I knew it was there." I said trying to explain it the best way I could.

"From here we will travel to many places and witness many things. I have brought you up in the ways of the Lord so I am counting on you to also spread God's message to those in whom you come into contact with." He told me as we sat looking up at the moon.

"Yes father I will......my Lord." I attempted to pay reverence, as it was awkward to call my father Lord.

"Ha ha you have known me all your life; there is no reason to be nervous now. I am still your father, and I still love you dearly just like my father loves me." He told me placing his hand on my shoulder.

I laughed with him in attempt to cut the awkwardness.

"I wanted to answer another one of your questions, the dark hooded figure that has been tormenting you. His name is satin." Father told me firmly.

"I understand, but why is he after me?" I asked feeling less important than father as to be a less important target for him.

"He always seeks the light, because he is the darkness. If he can dim that light, then that light cannot reach the dark places and shed truth where there are lies. He is also after me as well, for I feel that I will see him soon." Father explained.

"What do I do while you are away father?" I asked earnestly.

"Pray my child, pray and fast and read the scriptures so that you may further enable your light to shine." He told me.

"I will miss you." I told him as I began to cry.

"I will miss you as well my son." He replied with tears in his eyes as well.

Mother walked over to us and saw that we were crying.

"What is wrong?" She asked with concern yet again.

"I do the work that is prepared for me to do. But it is never easy to leave my family even though I know I must." He explained to her.

"I love you, and I understand." Mother said sobbing.

We sat underneath the moonlight the entire night while the others slept just talking. The topics were not destiny related or about what God has in store but yet of simple things, good memories, and just good old fun. The next morning when everyone awoke, father was preparing to leave. Grandmother went and hugged him tightly.

"Go and do your Father's work, we will be here when you return." She said sternly trying to hide her watering eyes.

"Yes ma'am, I will." He told her as his grip on her tightened.

For some reason I remembered that Naomi had given me that note back in Nazareth that I had forgot to read. I quickly opened it as the rest of our group said their temporary goodbyes to father. The note read;

"Yeshai, I know I am not the easiest person to get along with but you put up with me anyway. I always have a good time with you, even if we are not doing anything fun together. As you know I do not show emotion too well but thinking about when we sat on the roof of the temple that day really made me miss you when you left. And the thought of you leaving again hurts, so when you read this letter know that you are my best friend and I do really care about you. See you next time big head."

-Love Naomi

I shoved the letter back into my pocket and watched her hug my father. When she turned to look at me, I think she knew I had read her letter. I did not even realize I was crying, and so she came over to hug me as well.

"You just read the letter didn't you?" Naomi sarcastically asked.

"Yea I did." I calmly replied.

"Ugh, don't let it go to your head, or I will beat you the whole time your father is away." She warned me.

"I wouldn't have it any other way." I laughed.

After everyone said goodbye father turned to all of us and waived.

"I shall see you all soon, but until then love each other as I love each of you." *Jesus said as he turned around and began walking off into the wilderness until his figure was out of view.*

I watched my father walk away, and even though I could not feel him physically in that moment, I felt closer to him than ever. After he passed from view, I looked to the sky and realized who God was in relation to me and felt honored and motivated to do the work my father had instructed me to do. I am the son of Jesus Christ, the Messiah. Sent to do the work of his Father, so I must also work; for I am the Descendant.

**Truth comes in many shapes and forms, but when you obtain truth do not just hold on to it yet pass it on. Truth is a light that must be shared through the darkness to bring others into its light. God is the truth, and his light shines brightly. The enemy will try and dim that light trough lies and deceit but always remember that you can overcome that darkness by seeking the light because Christ is truth.**
**-Prophet**

"And if you belong to Christ, then you are Abraham's descendants, heirs according to promise."

Galatians 3:29

About the Author

Prophet (Jamal Johnson) is a poet, songwriter, Christian Hip Hop artist and author who now lives in Valparaiso, Florida. Born in Chicago, Illinois, he proudly serves in the United States Military. Although only publishing his first novel "The Descendant" with Xlibris Publishing Company, his passion for literature complimented by his love for music undoubtedly calls for future success. Prophet's poetry has been published in both the William's Poems anthology of poetry and the Chicago Poetry Association's poetry showcase novel in 2005. He has released two recording albums and his music has been praised by multiple sources to include the MusicMoney Corporation. Angela Barrett of the Chicago Public Schools Teachers Group said, "He is the next Langston Hughes." Prophet is eager to establish himself as an author and artist. He hopes his work will influence the lives of others through the Gospel, but his main focus is to make disciples.

CPSIA information can be obtained
at www.ICGtesting.com
Printed in the USA
BVOW09*0929070218
507514BV00008B/53/P